I AM
FARTACUS

Electric Boogerloo

**FIND OUT HOW CHUB'S
ADVENTURE BEGAN IN**

I Am Fartacus

I AM
FARTACUS

Electric Boogerloo

MARK MACIEJEWSKI

ALADDIN **MAX**

NEW YORK   LONDON   TORONTO   SYDNEY   NEW DELHI

This book is a work of fiction. Any references to historical events, real people, or real places are used fictitiously. Other names, characters, places, and events are products of the author's imagination, and any resemblance to actual events or places or persons, living or dead, is entirely coincidental.

ALADDIN MAX

Simon & Schuster Children's Publishing Division

1230 Avenue of the Americas, New York, New York 10020

First Aladdin MAX edition July 2018

Text copyright © 2018 by Mark Maciejewski

Cover illustration copyright © 2018 by Dan Widdowson

Also available in an Aladdin hardcover edition.

All rights reserved, including the right of reproduction in whole or in part in any form.

ALADDIN and related logo are registered trademarks of Simon & Schuster, Inc.

ALADDIN MAX is a trademark of Simon & Schuster, Inc.

For information about special discounts for bulk purchases, please contact Simon & Schuster Special Sales at 1-866-506-1949 or business@simonandschuster.com.

The Simon & Schuster Speakers Bureau can bring authors to your live event. For more information or to book an event, contact the Simon & Schuster Speakers Bureau at 1-866-248-3049 or visit our website at www.simonspeakers.com.

Book designed by Laura Lyn DiSiena

The text of this book was set in Janson.

Manufactured in the United States of America 0618 OFF

10 9 8 7 6 5 4 3 2 1

Library of Congress Cataloging-in-Publication Data

Names: Maciejewski, Mark, author.

Title: I am Fartacus : electric Boogerloo / Mark Maciejewski.

Other titles: Electric Boogerloo

Description: First Aladdin MAX edition. | New York : Aladdin MAX, 2018. |

Summary: Chub and The Arch are accused of stealing a sculpture of their school mascot and will be expelled by the strict new principal if they, aided misfit friends, old and new, cannot produce it in forty-eight hours.

Identifiers: LCCN 2017049182 (print) | LCCN 2017059575 (eBook) |

ISBN 9781481464246 (eBook) | ISBN 9781481464222 (pbk) | ISBN 9781481464239 (hc)

Subjects: | CYAC: Lost and found possessions—Fiction. | Interpersonal relations—Fiction. |

Popularity—Fiction. | Middle schools—Fiction. | Schools—Fiction. | Humorous stories. |

BISAC: JUVENILE FICTION / Social Issues / Bullying. | JUVENILE FICTION /

Humorous Stories. | JUVENILE FICTION / Social Issues / Friendship.

Classification: LCC PZ7.1.M2453 (eBook) |LCC PZ7.1.M2453 Iaak 2018 (print) |

DDC [Fic]—dc23

LC record available at https://lccn.loc.gov/2017049182

For Dad.

I love you, man.

CHAPTER 1

It's almost impossible to do a move called *Repulse Monkey* without giggling, but a summer of tai chi has taught me this: if I want to harness the strength hidden within me, I can't laugh every time something sounds like the name of a Norwegian rock band.

Last spring, after I got into (and back out of) some trouble at school, my dad made me take up a sport to burn off all my extra energy and build my character. My parents and I moved to the U.S. from Poland when I was little, and they don't get out much, so when I suggested tai chi my dad didn't think martial arts qualified as a sport. But when he found out it was free, he instantly became a fan. My dad likes tai chi because it's economical. I like it because it helps me focus the energy I used to use plotting against the Arch. Also because I'm as athletic as a three-legged turtle.

I meet my group every weekday morning at the park a few blocks from my house. I'm the youngest person there by sixty years, which is fine with me. Kids my age like to do a lot of running and jumping and throwing, which means sweating. Who needs that when I can keep my dad off my back and never get my heart rate over seventy-five?

The next move after *Repulse Monkey* is *Grasp the Bird's Tail*, but you can't go right into it. First you have to do a transition move called *Hold the Ball*. If I can get through that one, I'm usually fine for the rest of my practice. Mrs. Cheung gives me a kind smile while demonstrating perfect form. Tai chi is basically martial arts in superslow motion; I smile back, imagining her kicking a mugger's butt with her moves sped up ten times.

All this meditation has given me plenty of time to ponder the last school year. Last spring my friends and

I formed a Cadre, kind of like our own personal Justice League, to take down my former best friend turned nemesis, Archer Norris. After he stopped hanging out with me in second grade, he started acting like a totally different person. Suddenly he became Mr. Popular at school. He got taller quickly and became a hero because he was awesome at every sport he tried. He even gave himself the stupid nickname "the Arch," like he was some sort of celebrity or something.

And the reason he dumped our friendship? I used some chemicals from my dad's dry cleaning shop to kill the head lice we'd both gotten—and it ended up leaving me a bald second grader. The hair still hasn't grown back.

When all was said and done last year, my Cadre and I ended up exposing the Arch's illegal poker career and stopping a major embezzling scheme he was running to pay for it all.

Obviously, the final months of the school year were awkward between us, to say the least.

The problem is, once it was all out on the table, we didn't have anything to antagonize each other about.

It's not like we instantly became best friends or any-thing, but our old archenemy spark definitely cooled, and neither of us seemed to know if we should trust each other again. We saw each other a couple times over the summer; once at the Clairmont, the old-fashioned movie theater my cousin Jarek manages, on the opening night of *League of Honor*, and once at this very park. Archer, Troy, Nate, and a bunch of other athletic kids were bashing each other's brains in, fighting over a football, as I practiced *Carrying the Tiger over the Mountain* with my tai chi friends. My heart sped up when our eyes met, but he just looked away and went back to his game. Who knows? Maybe he didn't actually see me.

The truth is, years of battling the class hero sort of made me into the school villain. I can't blame anyone else; it was kind of fun being infamous. But I've been playing the villain game so long, I don't know how else I'm supposed to keep myself occupied at school this year.

There's scuffling behind me. Herman usually falls over trying to do the move called *Snake Creeps Through the Grass*, which is hilarious, and I want to finish my last session before the first day of school on a high note, so I strain my eyes to the side, hoping to witness a clumsy topple. But it isn't the sound of the only person in Seattle less coordinated than me eating a grass sandwich; instead, it's a pasty kid in tight jeans and a button-down shirt weaving his way through the maze of elderly martial artists.

My best friend, Moby, rushes toward me, side-stepping my tai chi friends like he's negotiating a blackberry patch.

"Chub!" he calls.

I ignore him, practicing my focus. Then he's standing right next to me.

"There you are," he says, panting from the climb up the small knoll where we practice. "You're harder to spot with all these other bald people here."

I nod my head toward a park bench, hoping he'll go wait quietly for me to finish. Like everything else someone's ever tossed Moby in his life, he doesn't catch the hint.

He shakes my shoulder like he's trying to wake me up. "Hellooo?"

I glance at Mrs. Cheung again. Her smile is still there, but the kindness meter is dialed back about three clicks. She speaks slowly. "Does your friend want to try tai chi?"

"No thanks," Moby says. "My parents don't let me have caffeine."

I slap my head, then relax out of the pose I'm holding. My concentration is shot; practice is finished for the day. I lead Moby over to the bench where I left my bag.

"You're early," I say, stripping off my silk uniform. My school clothes underneath are a little soggy with sweat, but no worse than usual. "Did you skip your bathroom session this morning?"

Moby digs a handful of denim out of his butt. "No, my parents switched the salad greens from romaine to kale, so it doesn't take as long."

I shudder at the idea of Moby being even more "regular" than he already is.

"That's cool," I say.

"I guess," he says, shrugging. "I've got lots more free time now."

Moby's parents buy him a new wardrobe at the beginning of every school year. Last year the stuff they bought him made him look like a dad from the 1950s. This year the look is slightly more current, but it's still obvious a kid didn't pick it out.

"What's up with your pants?"

Moby looks down at his outfit. "They're skinny jeans."

"But you aren't skinny."

"It's a fashion thing," he says, picking some imaginary lint off the pants.

"I thought they were just too small for you."

He laughs. "That's what I thought too."

Whatever. If he wants to go to school looking like an overstuffed bratwurst, that's his deal. I'll stick to 501s and T-shirts.

As distracting as Moby's new clothes are, my mind is really on what's going to happen when I run into the Arch at school. Will he leave me alone, or will things go right back to the way they were before, with him and his friends making fun of me and me and my friends doing everything we can to bring him down?

We leave the park and head west up the sidewalk toward Alanmoore Middle School. Moby chatters about his new wardrobe, but all I can think about is what will be waiting for me at school. I have to stay off the principal's radar this year, no matter what. My dad thinks growing up in America has made me soft. He's itching for an excuse to send me back to Poland for a summer of hard labor on my Uncle Stan's potato farm. I used up every bit of luck I had avoiding deportation last year and I don't think I can deal with that kind of stress again. I've given up my desire to be infamous; this year I just want to be a normal student.

I spot Shelby's front door from a block away. I figure she'll be sitting on the front porch in one of her Grammie's dresses waiting for us, but the front porch is empty. As we approach the house I slow down a little bit. I'm not going to knock on her door and invite her to walk to school with us, but if she comes out when we pass I guess it's okay if she joins us.

We're almost safely past when she flies out the front door and careens down the porch steps, noodly arms and legs thrashing in every direction at once.

"Guys, wait up!" she calls, even though we've already stopped to wait for her.

I take a step back as she gets close, so she doesn't accidentally slap me with one of her flailing flamingo flippers. "What are you so excited about?"

"It's the first day of school!" she practically sings.

I stare at Moby, who looks as confused by her answer as I am. "So?"

"So!" she yells. Moby flinches but doesn't run away. "So, new faces, new opportunities. This is a very exciting day!"

"What are you talking about? We've all gone to school together for years. It's just another nine months of government-mandated torture."

Shelby dashes in front of us and stops, blocking the sidewalk. "You guys didn't read the letters the school district sent home over the summer, did you?"

Moby and I look at each other. I do my best to appear ashamed for not reading the letters. I hold it for a second, but then we both lose it and burst into laughter.

"What kind of kid reads a letter from the school district?" I say, wiping away tears.

Moby shakes with laughter. "Who—*gasp*—who *reads* over the summer?"

I dry my eyes and look at Shelby. Her hands on her hips tell us she is not amused. She actually looks kind of hurt. Apparently *she* is the kind of kid who reads those letters.

"Shelby," I say, regaining my composure, "I'd rather eat a bowl of toenails than read a letter from the school."

She folds her arms over her chest. "Well, then I guess you guys are in for a few surprises today," she says. She spins on her heel and storms away down the sidewalk.

I don't like the sound of that. My activities at school have always required me knowing exactly what is going on. But I'm planning on turning over a new leaf this year, so maybe it won't be that big of a deal if I'm not on top of everything.

I know one thing for sure: there's no way I'm going to chase Shelby down and give her the satisfaction of hearing me ask what those letters had to say.

Moby and I don't talk the rest of the way to school.

The only sounds are the cars whizzing by and the rhythmic *shwip-shwip-shwip* of Moby's skinny jeans rubbing together as he walks.

Alanmoore looks the same as it always does, kinda like a church and a mental institution had a baby. Pangs of nervousness like I felt in the past when I saw my school flare up in my guts. *This year is going to be different*, I remind myself.

I decide to start seventh grade by walking in the building's front door instead of the back, like I always have. Moby doesn't question the move; he just follows me.

We pause in the stone entryway.

"It's a new year," I say.

"I know," Moby replies.

"Let's make it a good one."

He shrugs. "Okay."

I reach for the knob. "Here's to staying out of trouble." But as I touch it a tiny blue spark stings my finger. "GOAT FARTS!!!" I scream, more surprised than actually hurt by the static shock.

"The Colonel says that's from scuffing your feet

on the ground like a dirtbag when you walk," Moby explains. Moby's grandpa is a retired army colonel who lives with them. He can spot a dirtbag from miles away.

I'm not going to kid myself. I might know things are going to be different, but this building probably feels like it owes me a little payback for years of pranks, like stink bombs and plugged toilets. I can take whatever bad karma I have coming my way.

I grasp the knob again; this time there's no shock. The heavy door swings inward on squeaky iron hinges and we step into the main hallway for the first time as seventh graders.

The echo of first-day chatter is deafening. We weave our way through the knot of incoming sixth graders and make our way to the back staircase that leads to our lockers on the second floor. I think about what Shelby said about new faces. I don't recognize anyone here, but it doesn't surprise me, since they were all in grade school somewhere else last year.

On the second floor I make a beeline for my locker. Shelby's comment is starting to bug me, and I want to drop off my bag and find her to ask her what she meant. I slam the locker shut and scan the hallway. I do recognize some faces: student body secretary Sam Hardwick, Rooney Filbert, and that kid with one continuous eyebrow who everyone calls Bert (as in, "Hey Bert, where's Ernie?").

At the far end of the hall, in the middle of a crowd of high-fiving jocks, is my old nemesis. I watch him for a second, looking for some clue to whether I'm still looking at his phony persona, *the Arch*, or if he's back to just being plain old Archer Norris. From this far away it's hard to tell. He looks up from his welcoming committee and our eyes meet. I'm about to duck into the crowd and hide when something odd happens. Arch quickly averts his eyes, and then he slips away, leaving several hands un-high-fived.

How un-Archlike.

Then I spot another face I recognize noodling her way through the crowd toward us. Apparently Shelby's done punishing us.

"Did you figure it out yet?" she says smugly.

"What? The new faces thing?"

She smirks.

"Yeah, a bunch of sixth graders, big deal."

She folds her arms again. "Not just that. Since you aren't going to figure it out on your own, and since I forgot to bring the letter with me, I'll just tell you."

Moby and I put on our most uninterested looks.

"Okay, do you guys remember when that levy for school funding failed last November?"

"Oh yeah," I say.

Shelby's look brightens.

"But I always remember that as the day I didn't care about boring stuff like school levies, instead."

Her brow flattens into a line. "Anyway, the vote was a real nail biter at fifty-two percent—"

I wave my hand to cut her off. "So it failed, and—?"

"And they had to shut down Trondson Middle School, which meant they had to rezone the district."

I have never been less interested in a series of words than the ones coming out of Shelby's mouth right now. "So?"

"So, one third—well, thirty-six percent of the students, to be exact—now have to go here!"

I know two things about TMS: having them out of

the picture will make Coach Farkas happy, since they are our track team's biggest rivals; and Trondson has a reputation as a pretty rough place. Who knows which third of their students we got—the good third, the bad third, or the ugly third?

I'll have to swing by and get the scoop from Principal Mayer later. Last year, our principal was involved in the same poker league as the Arch. The league was run by a crooked bookie named Mace who loaned people money and then cheated to win it back from them. Moby won second place in the regional tournament as part of our plan to take the Arch down. We ended up using some of the money he won to pay off both his and Mr. Mayer's debts to Mace, so you could say Mr. Mayer owes me one.

For now, I just sweep the hallway one more time to see if I can spot any obvious transplants. I can't lie; I've spent the last few years so focused on my anti-the-Arch mission, I haven't really gotten to know many of my classmates. I'm about to stamp Shelby's surprise with a big *Who cares?* when something catches my eye.

The first thing I notice is the hair: straight-cut

bangs framing porcelain cheeks. Then the eyes: big, black, shiny, and almond-shaped, covering half of the face. I lose my breath. I didn't think this would happen to me until I was much older, but here I am on the first day of seventh grade face to face with the comic of my dreams.

I'm standing a few short steps away from a mint copy of the legendary comic book writer Tatsuo Kobayashi's masterpiece, *Ronin Girl* number one. I might faint. I don't recognize the girl holding it; she must be new to Alanmoore. She actually looks a little bit like Ronin Girl, except she's wearing leggings and a T-shirt instead of a samurai kimono. I look back at the comic, which is properly sleeved. This kid knows her stuff. I cock my head to read the title for one hundred percent confirmation, and I have to stifle an involuntary squeal when I realize I can't even read it because it is written in the original Japanese!

Shelby snaps me out of my trance.

"Ew!" she says, poking my shoulder. "Stalk much?"

She clearly doesn't understand the subtle difference between stalker and connoisseur.

I must meet this person and find out how she came into possession of the Holy Grail of rare Japanese comics. She puts the book in her locker. Now's my chance to introduce myself. Out of habit, I scan the hallway for the Arch before stepping into the crowd. I spot him instantly. His hand is in his locker, but his eyes are on something else. He's locked on to the new student too, only I don't think he's interested in her comic book.

He breaks his creeper gaze and looks at me, giving me a small smile I can't interpret. He nods and then disappears into the river of kids looking for their first class. When I look back to Ronin Girl's locker, she's gone. Our fateful meeting will have to happen some other time, hopefully before the Arch gets to her.

I turn to Shelby and do a bad job of hiding my giddiness. "This is a pretty good surprise."

She pushes her glasses up and gives me a disappointed look. "Oh, there's more," she says.

She's about to spill it when the squelch of the PA speakers splits the air. We all quiet down to hear Mr. Mayer's first "Good mooooorning, Alanmoore" of the new school year.

Only the voice over the speaker isn't Mr. Mayer's. It's a woman's voice, and there is no cheerful "Good morning."

"This is your new principal, *Mizzzz* Lockhart."

Instinctively, I look over at Moby. He does not like change of any kind, and this is the sort of thing that can send him scurrying off in search of a hiding spot.

The icy voice on the PA continues. "I look forward to meeting each and every one of you in the near future. Most of you in the halls." She pauses. "But no doubt some of you will insist on meeting me in my office instead. I'm sure you know who you are."

My scalp flushes. All of my tai chi Zen is officially spent.

Shelby gives me the smug look again. "—And that's the rest of the surprise."

CHAPTER 2

Last year Mr. Mayer couldn't afford for the school board to find out about his poker habit, so he kept me quiet by letting me serve my detention in solitary confinement, aka: the library. But just because my relationship with Mr. Mayer was built on a foundation of blackmail and the threat of mutual destruction doesn't mean I didn't like the guy. Our arrangement allowed me to carry out my plots against the Arch without getting in serious trouble, while I provided him the ability to keep his job by not tattling about his gambling to the school board. It wasn't the ideal relationship, but it worked for us. I suppose what I liked most was that it was comfortable. I knew exactly where I stood with Mr. Mayer, even if I was usually standing in a giant pot of knee-deep hot water.

Alanmoore getting a new principal changes everything. I don't have the energy to train a new one to do things the way I like them done. Not that Mizzzz Whatever sounds especially trainable, anyway. Then again, I'm not planning on getting in trouble this year, so hopefully, it won't be that much of an issue.

Still, you can be sure I'll open every single piece of mail from the school district from now on.

The smart play is to do a little recon on our new principal and determine if she is really as tough as she wants us to think or if she's just trying to make a scary first impression. I don't want to get myself on her radar right away, so I drop a note in one of the McQueens' lockers. I hang a paper clip from one of the vents in their locker door to let them know there's a message inside before I head off to my first class of the new year.

The McQueens are a set of triplets I use for special missions that I can't afford to have traced back to me. They prefer to work on a contract-by-contract basis, so they aren't official members of my Cadre. In the past they've plugged a lot of toilets and even blew one up with a cherry bomb as a distraction for a plot I was carrying out. The three of them share this old-fashioned cap, and only the one who's wearing it will speak. It takes a little getting used to, but who cares when you get three for the price of one?!

After spotting a *Ronin Girl* number one in the hall this morning, I'd hoped to spend the day figuring out how to get a look at it. But with the new principal making veiled threats during the announcements, I have more than enough to keep my mind busy during homeroom.

The morning's classes feel like they take forever. By the time the lunch bell rings I'm dying to get with the McQueens and send them on their first task of the year. I race down the stairs and out the back door as quickly as I can.

I wait and wait and wait with nothing but the marshy funk of the Dumpsters to keep me company, and before I know it the bell rings signaling the end of lunch. It isn't like them to miss a meeting. They all have access to the locker, so I'm pretty sure they got the message. Something must've come up. I'll just have to wait until after school to meet up with them.

It occurs to me that I have no idea what this Mizz Lockhart even looks like. I walk around to the front of the school so I can cruise by the principal's office and at least get a glimpse of her. As I approach the door, I slow my stroll and casually glance inside. The school secretary, Mrs. Osborne, taps away at her computer. She looks up when she senses my presence, but she just shakes her head and goes back to her work. Usually when she shakes her head at me it's out of disappointment, but this time it almost looks like a warning.

The door to Mr. Mayer's old office is open. I move to the opposite side of the hallway and slide into the hollow next to the large glass trophy case. I scan the interior of the office as best I can from my vantage point. I can't see the other side from here, so I slide down to the far end of the trophy case for a better view.

What I see sends my pulse into overdrive. All three McQueen triplets are standing off to the side of the desk, and their faces look like they've just seen a monster.

Besides the Arch, the triplets are the most unflappable kids in the whole school. No matter what kind of stunts they pull, they have the unique gift of never appearing guilty. But that isn't the case now. Now they look like three men who've been caught red-handed. And there's something else wrong with their appearance that I can't quite place.

All of their eyes shift toward the door. I think they've noticed me, and I press myself deeper into the shadow of the trophy case. But they aren't looking at me. They're watching the other person in the room, whom I can't see. Their eyes grow wide a moment before a pale hand wraps itself around the edge of the door like a daddy longlegs crawling out of a box. With a flick of the wrist, the door slams, sealing my friends inside. The last image I have is the terrified faces of the normally cool triplets. It isn't until the door is closed that I realize what else is wrong.

None of them is wearing the hat.

Moby and Shelby are already in their desks when I get to my math class. Julius "Sizzler" Jackson joined our Cadre and helped us take down the Arch last year. He used to be the fastest kid in school until the Arch joined the track team and stole the title. But people don't call him Sizzler because he's fast; they call him that because there are more food options available in his braces than there are at the Sizzler buffet. He shows up next and wedges his giant frame into the desk next to me. Mrs. Berry is chatting with another teacher in the hallway, so everyone takes advantage and carries on loud conversations.

Shelby spins around in her chair, smiles hello to Sizzler, and examines me.

"Where were you during lunch?" she says. "Did *she* get you?"

"No, *she* didn't get me," I say. "Why?"

Sizzler leans in. "I heard she pulled Derek Van Sant right out of English class today. They say when he came back at the end of the period he just sat in the corner crying."

Shelby gets a quizzical look. "Who's Derek Van Sant?"

"He's the high jumper from the track team," I say, looking back and forth between them. "He's also the kid who jumped up onstage with the water balloon during the Arch's campaign speech last spring."

Shelby points her finger at me. She says what I'm already thinking. "She's rounding up known trouble-makers. Trying to put the fear of God in them."

The terrified look on the McQueens' faces as she shut the door flashes in my mind.

"She got the McQueens," I say.

Moby and Shelby draw in sharp breaths. Sizzler shakes his head.

"What does she want?" Moby asks.

"Probably to prove how tough she is by crushing any trouble before it even has a chance to start. If she grabs one of us, we have to keep our mouths shut about the Cadre, agreed?"

They all nod.

"I wonder why she hasn't grabbed you yet," Moby says.

I've been wondering the same exact thing.

"Maybe Mr. Mayer didn't rat me out since I helped him with the Mace situation," I suggest.

Sizzler shakes his head. "Or maybe she's saving you for the grand finale."

I don't want to admit it, but that thought occurred to me, too. Maybe she's bringing in all the little fish one at a time and getting them to rat on me. Maybe she wants to be sure she's built a file on me and my activities before she sits me in the chair and puts the hot light in my face. She won't have to talk to too many people to get a complete list of every stink bomb, plugged toilet, and alleged arson incident I was involved in last year.

Then something occurs to me: What am I nervous about? Last year is over. I haven't done anything yet, nor do I intend to. Let her grab me if she wants; I've got nothing to hide.

When the final bell rings I race through the halls looking for three orange heads. I finally catch them in the parking lot.

"Guys!" I call.

They stop and then reluctantly turn around. None of them is wearing the talking hat.

"Where's your hat?"

Their eyes are red, and their jaws are slack. The trademark McQueen swagger is gone. Now they look like men who've just been handed a life sentence. They glance around, then one of them ushers me over to the Dumpsters. The other two post up as lookouts, and the third unzips his backpack. I expect him to pull out the old-fashioned newsboy hat they all share. Instead, he pulls out a homemade knit cap with a big yarn pompom on top.

I almost laugh, but they are clearly not amused, so I quickly wipe the smile off my face.

"What the heck happened to you guys in there?" I ask.

He can't look me in the eye. "She knows."

"Knows what?"

"Everything, or at least enough. She knows who you are, she knows you're the one to watch. She knows who your friends are. And she doesn't plan on letting you get away with anything!"

Is this the price of achieving infamy?

He continues. "She expels one kid a year as an example to anyone considering bad behavior. She has a file of all the kids she's taken out at other schools." He makes a face like he's going to be sick. "She showed it to us like it was some sort of trophy. She also told us she's already got a list of candidates here. Then she—" The words catch in his throat.

"What did she do to you?" I put a hand on his shoulder to let him know he's safe now.

"She took the hat, then she made us all talk."

How sick is this lady to put them through that?

"She said if we cause any trouble . . . ," he puts his closed hand to his mouth. "The hat goes in the incinerator. That's Grandpa McQueen's lucky hat! He wore it for all three of his not-guilty verdicts."

Who is this maniac? If I didn't know better, I'd say she's trying to start some kind of war. Obviously, any little slip on my part will give her the justification she needs to make me the example she is looking for.

It kills me to see them with their heads hung low. I walk the McQueen, Darby I think, out of the hollow behind the Dumpsters. Before we step out of the protective shadows, he removes the replacement cap and stuffs it in his backpack.

The other two give up their posts and flank their brother.

"I'm sure she's just trying to make an impression on her first day," I say, even though I have no idea if that's true. "Don't worry, I'm going to stay clean this year."

With the hat in the backpack, I don't take offense when none of them reply. They just nod slightly and look at the ground. I look down too, and my own shadow catches my eye. It's bigger than it should be— and it's getting taller.

Then my shadow grows one arm, and then another, each tipped with long, spidery fingers.

When I look up again, all I see are the backs of the triplets sprinting for the bus stop. I don't want to turn around. I know exactly what's there.

A voice like water dripping on dry ice hisses behind me.

"Mr. Trzebiatowski. We meet at last."

CHAPTER 3

You know those dreams where you're somewhere you've been a million times, but it's just different enough that you know something is wrong? Sitting in Mr. Mayer's old office with Mizz Lockhart gives me that feeling, only stronger.

The light coming in through the window glints off her steel-colored hair. It's short on the sides and longer on top, like Gozer the Gozerian from *Ghostbusters*. I half expect her eyes to flare red when she talks, but she doesn't say anything. She just sits broom-handle straight behind her desk and watches me. If Mr. Mayer was like a padlock with the combination written on the outside, this lady is like a jumbled-up Rubik's Cube encased in a block of ice.

This isn't going to be easy.

The Colonel says guilty people always talk first, so I settle into the wooden chair, drum my fingers on the armrest, return her gaze, and wait for her to say what she has to say.

After what feels like hours, but is probably only a minute, she shifts. Her chair squeaks as she leans forward. I brace for whatever psychological torture she's about to throw at me. No matter how heinous it may be, I promise myself not to end up crying in the corner, like Derek Van Sant.

"Tea?"

"Huh?"

She folds her hands on her desk and slowly says, "Would you like some tea?"

I know this trick. This is where the evil interrogator pretends like they're doing something nice, but then slips something in your drink, or takes it away before you can actually drink it so you know they're in control.

I prop my elbows on the chair and steeple my fingers. "No."

"No—what?"

"No tea," I say, stating the obvious.

"I think you mean, no thank you."

Maybe I do, but I'd rather get on with the interrogation.

She stands, walks to the corner, and fills a mug from a hot-water machine and then spoons some leaves into a little metal ball on a chain. She comes back to the desk and gently dunks the little metal thing in the mug.

I focus on the mug to avoid her gray-eyed gaze.

"I see you've noticed my Wahoolie," she says.

"Nope." I have no clue what a Wahoolie is.

She removes the little tea ball and sets it on a saucer. "My mug," she says, raising it for one-sided cheers.

She takes a slurpy sip and then sets the cup back down.

"You have a good eye. This is one of a kind."

I examine the mug. It looks like a miniature frozen tornado of vomit. "It's nice," I lie.

"It was a gift," she says. "From the artist himself."

Big deal—some five-year-old made her a craft project. And who names their kid Wahoolie? I glance around the office trying to avoid looking at her or her ugly little teacup. There's a poster on the wall that wasn't there last year. It's a framed banner for a gala at some art museum downtown. Suddenly I realize what a Wahoolie is. It's not a kid; it's this guy who lost his arm to a crocodile or something, and then took up glassblowing. He eventually became superfamous for it. Supposedly, he lives in Seattle now.

She slowly sips her tea and waits for me to be blown away by the name-drop.

I try to look as bored as possible. "Do you know him?"

I can almost hear the sound of a glacier cracking as she smiles.

"Oh yes," she says, looking lovingly at the mug. "We are—quite close."

Vomit rises in my throat at the thought of adults being "close." I need to get out of here and get to my parents' shop before they start to wonder what I've gotten into on the first day of school.

"It's a neat mug, Mrs. Lockhart—"

She interrupts. "—Mizz."

I fight the urge to ask how many zs that izzzz, but I don't want this to last any longer than it has to. "Sorry, Mizz Lockhart. But I need to get going."

"Oh, right. You're probably expected at the shop."

Ghost fingers drag across my neck. She knows way too much about me.

She looks at me over the top of the mug. "I'll have to stop in there soon to have my pantsuits pressed." Then she takes a long, loud sip.

I don't want her to see me sweat. Guilty people sweat. I remind myself I haven't done anything wrong.

"Well, it was nice to meet you," I say, putting my hands on the chair to push myself out of it.

Her eyes flick at me.

"Sit," she says like she's talking to a dog. "We haven't finished our tea." She picks up the mug and takes a long, wet slurp.

She sets down the mug, rolls up the sleeve of her blazer, and slips a coiled bracelet with a key chain attached to it off her wrist. "I always like to get to know my new students," she says. Her mouth smiles, but her eyes don't. "Especially ones I've heard so much about."

"Mmmhmm," I mumble.

She selects a key and unlocks the top drawer of her desk, then reaches in and pulls out a stack of papers.

I recognize the papers as soon as I see them. They're student files, four of them, and one of them is much thicker than the others. Without reading the name I know it's mine. She isn't the first principal to drop that file on the desk in front of me.

She sets mine aside and opens one of the others.

"Archer Norris." She shoves up her lower lip like she's impressed by what she sees. "Class president, captain of the football, basketball, and track teams. A small accident with some shoelaces and a lighter last year, but other than that quite an exemplary record. Do you know him?"

The temperature of my scalp goes up about twenty degrees. I nod carefully so I don't make the sweat on my forehead run into my eyes.

She closes the Arch's file and sets it aside, then opens the next one.

"Shelby Rose Larkin."

I break into a full-blown sweat. There's no way she has anything on Shelby.

Mizz Lockhart looks at Shelby's class photo attached to the folder with a paper clip, makes a sour face, then flips the file closed. "Perfect attendance, and an affinity for . . . let's say *vintage* . . . sweaters."

She takes another sip of her tea, then drums her fingers on the final folder. If her goal was to bring me in and scare me straight, mission accomplished.

She flips open the file too quickly for me to see the name. Her brow furrows in a confused look and she turns the file over as though it's empty. "Hmmm."

I don't want her to know how badly I want to know whose it is, but it's getting impossible to look uninterested.

After a pause she says, "Levi—Ethan—Dick."

My stomach falls and does a belly flop into the pool of sweat on my chair. I might deserve to be scrutinized, but Moby and Shelby, key members of the Cadre, are off-limits. I'm quickly switching from scared to angry.

"Mildly lactose intolerant, aaaand that's about it."

She looks up at me and our eyes meet.

"Have I upset you, Mr. Trzebiatowski?" she says with a hint of taunting in her voice. She lifts my file and drops it on the desk in front of her with a thump. "I don't think we need to go through all of this, do we?"

I shake my head but don't answer.

"You see, Mr. Trzebiatowski, I have a passion." *Another word you never want to hear an adult use.* "More of an obsession, really."

Ugly, overpriced drinking vessels? I think to myself, but what I say is, "Wahoolie?"

The corner of her eye twitches. "I'm obsessed with discipline and order. And I think you and your little . . . cabal are a threat to that order."

She leans back in her chair and steeples her fingers in front of her mouth.

Now seems like the perfect time to tell her I'm not planning on threatening her precious order at all, but after she threatened my friends like that, I don't want to give her the satisfaction. Instead I steeple my own fingers and return her gaze.

"I'm sure you've heard by now about my reputation," she says.

Every instinct tells me to keep my mouth shut, but I can't stop myself. "I've heard you like to expel kids to make sure everyone else stays in line."

She holds the mug up to the light. "Do you know what makes a Wahoolie a masterpiece? When he discovers an imperfection, he applies tremendous heat." Her eyes leave the mug and lock on me. "Then reshapes it until it's just the way he wants it."

I need to get out of here before she tries to melt me into a saucer to match her cup. "I don't think you need to fire up the blast furnace, Mizz Lockhart."

She sets down her cup and gives me a dubious look. "I shouldn't keep you. I'm sure there's something that needs starching or pressing somewhere, and as you can see, I have some . . . *work* to do as well."

I reach down to pick up my book bag, and when I look up, she's on my side of the desk.

She offers her hand and before I can stop myself, I shake it.

I try to pull my hand out of her icy grip, but she

doesn't let go. We lock eyes. "Shelly Mayer is long gone. Alanmoore is my world now," she says, her voice halfway to a whisper.

"Okay," I say, wrenching my hand free.

She pivots and goes back to her chair. She flips open a file on her desk and examines it.

Now I understand how Moby feels right before he pulls one of his famous disappearing acts. I want to be anywhere but here.

She glances up from the file and looks surprised I'm still there.

"That is all . . . for today."

I don't make her tell me twice. Mrs. Osborne gives me a look of pity as I walk out of the office and through the school's back door. Moby is waiting by the Dumpsters.

"What took you so long?" he says.

I hustle him off the school grounds before I answer. "She got me."

He looks me over like he expects a piece to be missing. "Are you okay?"

"Yeah," I say, even though my stomach is knotted up.

"What happened?"

I tell him the whole story, minus the part about his and Shelby's files, as he walks me to my parents' shop.

"Wait!" he says, putting his hand on my shoulder. "Mr. Mayer's name is Shelly?"

I was too nervous to laugh when she said it, but now we look at each other for a moment, then bust out laughing.

Moby laughs so hard he has to readjust his pants when he's finished. "Too bad you didn't know that last year. You could've gotten away with anything."

"Probably," I say. As she said, though, I'm in her world now, not Shelly Mayer's. The last thing on my mind is getting away with anything. In Mizz Lockhart's world, it's about basic survival.

"Wanna hang out later?" I say as we walk up to the shop. I partly want to hang with Moby, but I also want to run this whole situation by the Colonel.

"My parents are going to some appointment, but Grandpa and I will be home." This not only means very little supervision, but also something fried and delicious for dinner.

I say good-bye with a promise to come over as soon as I'm done helping my folks, then I go inside to see what awaits me.

My mother is all smiles when she sees me. "How was school, *rodzynek*?"

"School-y," I say, flinging my bag under the counter.

Thankfully, she doesn't have any annoying follow-up questions. "Papa is waiting in the back," she kisses me on the cheek as I pass.

My dad is working the single-buck press, sweating like a snowman in July. He stops when he sees me and wipes his face.

"How is school?" he asks.

I consider giving him the same answer I gave my mom, but I don't want to do anything to mess up my plans with Moby later.

"Pretty good." I rub my hands together to show him that's all I have to say and I'm ready to get to work.

He points at a rack of freshly dry-cleaned shirts. "Light day today, not many shirts."

I can be done pressing all of them in less than an hour. He must sense my relief at the small amount of work, because he quickly adds, "More time for homework."

Good old Dad. In a weird way, it's comforting to know that not everything is going to be different this year.

It takes me forty minutes to press and bag the shirts. I don't want to finish too quickly and risk getting a fresh assignment, so I grab my tai chi outfit and do a quick touch-up to take some of the stink out of it, then press it, put it on a hanger, and slip a plastic bag over it. Who knows how long it will be before I see my class again?

With all the work done, my parents don't give me any hassle about going to Moby's when I use the magic word "study."

When I arrive, Mr. Dick yanks the front door open, smiling like he's in some sort of pageant.

"Jetski!"

"Mr. Di—I mean, Jason," I say.

"Get your butt in here, man. We made a treat for you guys."

I pray that the smell assaulting my nose in the entryway is not *the treat*.

The Colonel nods to me as I walk into the kitchen. I nod back just as Mrs. Dick wraps me in one of her hugs.

"How was your first day of seventh grade?" she asks.

I shrug, tired of coming up with different ways to answer the same question. What do parents expect kids to say when they ask that?

She opens the oven, releasing a cloud of the rancid smell I caught in the hallway.

"Did you meet the new principal?"

I shoot a look at Moby, who shakes his head. "Um, no."

"Probably better that you didn't," Jason says. He chucks my shoulder and laughs.

The Colonel says, "Well, you guys don't want to be late. How much longer on the mouse caca?"

4 • MARK MACIEJEWSKI

"It's *moussaka*, and it'll be done in ten minutes," Mrs. Dick says. "But let it cool; you don't want to burn your tongue on a piece of eggplant."

The Colonel shakes his head. "I guarantee that won't happen."

Moby and I follow his parents to the front door and then watch as they pull out of the driveway. When the car disappears around the corner, Moby calls, "They're gone!"

The Colonel pokes his head in the family room. "You know what to do." He whips his index finger around like a twister.

Twenty minutes later, the moussaka is in the disposal and the pizza the Colonel ordered earlier arrives. I take a couple of slices, but the Colonel stacks extras on my plate like a delicious Jenga tower. "Can't have any evidence. Leave no man behind." We go to the table and dig in. "New CO, huh?" the Colonel says around a mouthful of half-chewed pizza.

"What's a CO?" I ask.

Moby chokes down a bite. "Commanding officer. He means Ms. Lockhart."

"Oh yeah. We got a new principal."

"I heard something about that. Old guy got fired. They brought in some hotshot lady to whip that place into shape."

Am I the only one who didn't know about this? "How'd you hear about it, sir?"

"I don't remember, some website. Pass the hot pepper flakes."

Moby rolls his eyes. "He checks up on the school board sometimes to make sure they aren't changing the history curriculum."

The Colonel shakes half the flakes in the little plastic cup onto a slice. "Last I checked America is eight and oh, with one tie. I just want to make sure they don't mess with our record."

Moby and I trade looks.

"I wouldn't worry about the new principal," he says. "She might come out of the gate like a rabid dog, but once she finds her cull, she'll settle down."

I don't know what that word means, but the sound of it makes me lose my appetite.

"What's a cull?" Moby asks.

The Colonel sets down his pizza, takes a deep breath, and wipes sweat off his forehead. "It's the oldest trick in the book. When you become the new boss, the best way to make sure nobody steps out of line is to make an example of somebody right away. You cull out the troublemaker." He wipes his hands together. "No more trouble."

My scalp is sweating, even though I haven't touched the peppers.

"What if there isn't a troublemaker?" I ask.

"Oh, someone always stands out," he says with a chuckle.

My plan to lie low is looking smarter by the minute. If I don't give her a reason, she'll have to find someone else to be her cull. My appetite makes a little comeback and I pick up a slice of Hawaiian.

"And if nobody volunteers, you just pick the guy with the reputation."

CHAPTER 4

A cull sounds like a type of fish to me, which is probably why I have nightmares about hanging upside down while Mizz Lockhart poses next to me like a she's just landed a prize marlin.

The next morning, I trudge to class feeling the way I had last year, when a single misstep could've gotten me sentenced to a summer on my Uncle Stan's potato farm in Poland. Today Moby's jeans aren't just too small; this pair has studs on them too. His butt sounds like the world's biggest pepper grinder as he slides in to the desk next to me. Everyone turns and looks, but I hardly notice. When you're bald in seventh grade, people turn and look at you a lot. Besides, people are always turning to see what sound Moby's butt is making now.

Moby rocks back and forth, clacking his beaded pockets on the chair until I put a hand on his arm and make him stop.

"What?" He looks hurt. "If you move like this, the big beads kinda give you a massage." He stares at me like he just saw a vampire. "You okay, Chub?"

"I didn't sleep well last night." I let go of his arm and put my head on my desk.

"That pizza tore me up too."

I consider telling him about the files yesterday in Lockhart's office, but I decide to leave him in ignorant bliss as long as possible. There's no reason for both of us to be completely stressed out, especially since I'm the one she really wants.

Shelby glides into the room with Sizzler and they take the desks we saved for them. I nod hello, then put my head back on the desk.

"Did she getcha?" Shelby grabs my shoulder to startle me and it works. I go from almost asleep to completely awake in less than a second.

"Oh, she got him all right." Moby shakes his head.

Shelby suddenly looks concerned. "What the heck did she say to . . ."

But I don't hear the rest of her question because someone behind her catches my eye.

Ronin Girl scurries into the room clutching her books to her chest. She sits at the desk closest to the radiator in the back corner of the classroom.

My head swims. Does she have *it* with her? I crane my neck to examine her stack of books. I don't see it. She's probably keeping it in her locker so nobody bumps into it in the hall and damages one of the corners.

Smart.

Shelby snaps her fingers in front of my face, bringing me out of my trance. "What is your deal?"

"Huh?"

She traces my gaze across the room and finds Ronin Girl at the other end of it. Shelby makes sure I see her eyes roll before she folds her arms and slumps back in her chair.

I put on my most wrongly accused face. "What?"

"Never mind." It's the second time she's caught me staring, but if she's willing to let it drop, so am I.

"Why are you staring at that new girl?" Moby spins in his seat to look at Ronin Girl too.

"I wasn't staring at her. I was just . . . checking for something."

Shelby lets out a snort and then refolds her arms hard enough to crack her pointy collarbone.

Thankfully, the bell rings and Shelby stops her chicken-wing-origami demonstration.

Our homeroom teacher this year, Mrs. Badalucco, waddles in just as the bell stops. It's hard to tell if her dress is tie-dyed or just ringed with stains from years of dried sweat. She makes it to the desk huffing and puffing and flops into the chair. Everyone likes Mrs. B, so we wait quietly as she pulls a roll of paper towels out of her bag and mops the sweat off her forehead. She's tearing off her third sheet to do her neck when the intercom squelches.

"This is Principal Lockhart." Lockhart's frostbit voice comes over the speaker.

Several students wince like someone's dragging a fork across a plate.

"There will be a mandatory assembly today during second period. The subjects will be discipline and school spirit. That is all." The speaker clicks and dies.

"So . . . you have that to look forward to." Mrs. B winks. She feels our pain.

I wrestle with a case of the sleepy head bobs and somehow live through homeroom. The bell wakes me with a start and I instinctively scan the room for Ronin Girl, but she apparently has ninja speed and used it to slip out.

"She left." Moby stuffs his books in his pack and shoulders it. He claps his hands and rubs them together Mr. Miyagi style. "Assembly time!"

We make our way to the gym and take our usual spot in the back row, hidden in the shadows of the rafters. I used to sit up here to avoid running into the Arch, but now it's just a good vantage point.

Mr. Mayer's podium is gone. Instead there's a small table in the middle of the basketball court.

Something sits on the table covered in a purple sheet.

I point at the mystery object. "What's that?"

Moby shrugs.

I try to make out the shape under the sheet, but no matter how hard I stare it doesn't make any sense. Then the gym goes silent except for the sound of a pair of heels clacking across the basketball court. Lockhart looks like what a pair of scissors would resemble if it could walk. She makes a line for the table and puts a hand on it.

She doesn't have a mic; how are we supposed to hear her?

"For those of you who have not met me yet, I am Mizzzzzzz Lockhart, and I am the new principal." Never mind. Her voice is as loud and clear as if it's coming through headphones in my ears.

Moby nods, impressed by Lockhart's unamplified volume.

"As noted in the announcements this morning, I called this assembly for two reasons. First: discipline."

A wave of grumbling rolls through the bleachers.

"Some of you have no doubt heard that I am quite strict." She pauses for another wave of grumbling that confirms what she just said. "I can assure you, most of what you've heard . . . is true."

Out of the corner of my eye I see a face. I glance over and the Arch is looking straight up at me. He raises his eyebrows, then turns back around.

"What was that about?" Moby says.

"I have no idea." I keep an eye on him in case he turns around again, but he doesn't.

"Disciplinary transgressions will NOT be tolerated." The word "not" makes everyone jump. "And at the end of this school year, my reputation will be intact."

Someone to my left *oooohs*, and a couple of kids giggle. Lockhart's head snaps toward the sound like a velociraptor and a hungry smirk splits her lips.

"Which brings us to part two of this assembly." Without taking her fingers off the table she walks around to the other side of it.

"A well-disciplined school is something to be

proud of. With that in mind, I present a very special gift from the studio of a local genius artist, Wahoolie." She pinches the top of the sheet and carefully lifts it off the object on the table.

When the thing is exposed, I'm no closer to identifying what the heck it's supposed to be. It looks like a three-foot-tall stack of purple snot.

Someone snorts and someone else giggles, but mostly people just chuckle quietly and look around to see if anyone else gets it. Nobody does.

I nudge Moby. "It looks like a deformed eggplant."

"It looks like a kangaroo," Moby says, like it's the most obvious thing in the world.

I rotate my head, but I don't see it. "Nope, eggplant."

Then Lockhart touches the base of the thing and a light comes on inside of it. It gives off a weak purple glow. "I give you an original hand-blown glass masterpiece, Electric Kangaroo!" She stands back and admires the glowing blob.

I still don't see a kangaroo, I see snot. I look at Moby, stunned.

"What?" he shrugs. "It is what it is."

I poke Moby with my elbow. "More like Electric *Boogerloo* if you ask me."

Moby chuckles.

A kid in the row closest to us must've heard me. "Ha! Boogerloo." He points at the thing and laughs, then someone farther down says it.

The comment spreads faster than pee in a swimming pool, because a few seconds later someone in the lower section calls out, "Electric Boogerloooooooo!" and the gym ripples with nervous laughter.

Lockhart takes her eyes off the Boogerloo and trains them on the heckler.

"Mr. Moles, please come see me in my office before you return to class."

I look down where the comment came from. All the kids surrounding Danny Moles lean away from him as Danny hangs his head.

"Where were we?" Lockhart continues. "Right. School spirit. When you pass this piece of art in the hall, let it fill you with pride at being an Alanmoore Kangaroo."

She pauses like she's waiting for applause, but it doesn't come.

"That is all," she says, like she can't believe we are still sitting there. She walks off the floor. Apparently part one of the assembly struck home, because everyone files out of the gym in too orderly of a fashion for a bunch of middle schoolers.

"Well, that was scary," I say once we are out of there.

"Why?" Moby shuffles along with the crowd. "Just don't do anything wrong and you'll be fine."

"I hope so."

I spot a glimpse of Ronin Girl's straight black hair cutting through the crowd toward her locker. This is finally my chance to get her alone and ask where she got an original-language edition of one of the rarest comics around.

"I'll see you at lunch, Mobe." I peel off and push through the crowd after her.

I take the stairs a little too fast and have to wait at the top to dry my scalp before I meet my destiny. When it's dry enough, I stroll around the corner into the empty hallway.

I look to her locker, and what I see rips my guts out through my belly button. Ronin Girl is already talking to someone else and giggling. The Arch leans on the locker next to hers. He smiles a little when he sees me. But the thing that crushes me is that she's showing him the comic that's meant for me.

CHAPTER 5

Sizzler sits at the lunch table inhaling two-dimensional slices of cafeteria pizza. Shelby enjoys a bag of dried apple slices, and Moby polishes off the one piece of moussaka we left in the pan so his mom wouldn't get suspicious. I pick at a bag of Sour Patch Kids, but they don't even make my eye twitch or anything. Ever since I saw the Arch reading *Ronin Girl* in the hallway, nothing has any flavor.

"You mad, Chub?" Sizzler holds up a slice of the paper pie. "Have some pizza."

I wave it off. If candy doesn't help, I doubt pizza will either. Sizzler doesn't give me a chance to change my mind. The pizza disappears into his mouth like a stormtrooper down the sarlacc pit. He licks some Cheetos-colored grease off his fingers and turns to Moby. "What's up with him?"

Moby puts down his spork, wipes his hands on his napkin, and gives me a concerned look. "He's been like this since he came out of Lockhart's office yesterday."

Sizzler takes on Moby's concerned look. "What'd she say to you in there?"

I fish in the bag of candy to avoid eye contact. "Basically what she said in the assembly." *Not technically a lie.*

Sizzler rips out a burp that sounds like his pizza is going to make an encore appearance. "That lady is scary."

Moby nods. I look at Shelby, who hasn't said a word since first period. She folds her hands on the table.

Sizzler apparently doesn't know better. "What do you think, Shelby?"

She smiles at the acknowledgment, then pushes up her glasses and aims her stare at me. Here comes the lecture.

"She knows you and Archer Norris were the two names on Mr. Mayer's watch list last year. That's why you're already on the top of hers."

"I have no idea what Archer is up to, but I haven't done anything to her."

She pushes up her glasses. "Think about it, Maciek. If she's going to expel someone to show the rest of the students that she means business, who better than one of the kids that everyone knows almost burned down the school last year? You guys have practically volunteered as the perfect candidates."

My scalp gets hot. She's probably right. This is all I need, on top of the Arch horning in on my rare-comic hookup.

Sizzler washes down a bite of pizza with some milk, then wipes his mouth on his sleeve. "Man, Trondson's gone. If you get kicked out of here you're gonna have to move to another district!"

Shelby gives him a dubious look. "Every child has a right to an education. They can't make you move. There are other options, like private school."

My parents can barely afford to keep their shop

open. There's no way they are going to pay for me to go to a fancy school if I get kicked out of a perfectly good free one. The image of the Arch raising his eyebrows at me during the assembly flashes to mind. It didn't mean anything to me then, but maybe he'd already done the math on what would happen if one of us got kicked out. Maybe that eyebrow was his way of saying *game on*.

I jump up from the table and toss the rest of my candy to Sizzler. I have to find the Arch before he does anything stupid.

I'm in the hall outside the cafeteria before I realize Moby is following me.

"Where are we going, Chub?"

I know he won't stop asking until I explain, so I do. "Archer Norris is the class president. There's no way he'll be the cull if he stays out of trouble."

"Uh-huh."

"If Shelby's right and it's either him or me, I only have two options. Either do something to make sure that it's him and not me . . ."

Moby smiles an eager smile.

". . . Or I call a truce to keep us both safe."

The grin disappears, replaced by the frown he gets when he doesn't know where the closest bathroom is. "So what are you going to do?"

"I have to assume he's thinking the same thing I am." I take a deep breath. "So I'm going to talk to him and figure out if he's up to something. Then I'll decide."

I walk again, but Moby doesn't follow me. He's standing in the same spot and looking at me like I'm crazy.

"What, Mobe?"

"You want a truce? With the Arch?"

I walk back to where he's standing so I don't have to yell down the hall. "It would be better than having him working against me, wouldn't it?"

Moby thinks it over. "What about the first thing you said, about doing something to him first? You don't trust him, do you?"

The idea of striking first has a certain nostalgic appeal, but I need to figure out what he's thinking before I decide to make a huge move. "I never said I trusted him."

Moby thinks about it for a second, then sighs. "Okay, but don't say I didn't warn you."

We start walking again. The Arch is probably eating lunch in the courtyard with the other jocks. When we pass the trophy case, a pale purple glow catches my eye.

I'm face to face with the Boogerloo. Even up close, I don't see a kangaroo. I shake my head at the thing. How are we supposed to feel pride over something that looks like a stalagmite of ogre loogies?

I scan the hall. "You know what I think, Mobe?"

"That we're lucky to be able to enjoy such beautiful art in a public school?"

I stare at him. "No! I think somebody should steal this stupid thing and teach old Lockhart a lesson."

He slowly turns his head toward me. "I thought you were trying to stay out of trouble."

I take one last look at the thing and then start walking again. "Not me, just someone. She can't threaten us like this when we haven't even done anything yet."

"And you want to steal a really expensive piece of art to show her she's wrong about you being a troublemaker?"

I laugh. "Probably not the best plot I ever invented."

Moby just shakes his head.

The Arch isn't in any of the usual spots with any of the usual suspects. There are only a few minutes left during lunch, when a sickening thought hits me. What if he's somewhere alone with Ronin Girl reading the comic? I change course and cut up the old back stairs toward her locker. When I get to the second-floor landing I slow down so I don't look crazy running around the corner. Moby catches up a second later, his V-neck T-shirt blotched with sweat. I creep to the corner and peek around it.

There's someone in the hall.

"What do you see?" Moby whispers loud enough to start an avalanche.

I wave my hand to keep him quiet, then take another look. It's her, and this time the Arch is nowhere in sight.

Her locker door is open, blocking her view, so we slip out of the landing and walk quietly down the hall toward her. The last thing I want to do is act all weird and scare her away.

We are a few feet from her locker when she moves the door and sees us. But she doesn't run; she just smiles. I quickly check the books in her arms and see a familiar plastic sleeve between two textbooks.

This is the moment I've been dreaming about.

"I'm Chub." I shove my hands in my pockets.

She gives us a confused look.

"This is Moby."

Ronin Girl looks at me, then at Moby. "No English." She shakes her head.

"We know English too," Moby says.

I resist the urge to smack my forehead. "She means she doesn't speak English." Maybe her and the Arch weren't having a deep discussion after all.

I pull my hands out of my pockets and show them to her.

She gives me a suspicious look.

Then I plaster a smile on my face and slowly point toward the plastic sleeve. She hugs her books tighter and takes a step back.

"No, no. I just want to talk."

She looks back and forth between me and Moby.

Moby tries to help. "Don't worry, he's not a weirdo or anything."

Ronin Girl looks at me as though I can interpret.

"Why don't you try charades?" Moby offers.

It might work. I don't know any samurai moves to show her I'm talking about *Ronin Girl*, so I try the only martial art I know. I go into a tai chi pose called Crane Spreads Its Wings.

Still holding the pose, I point toward the comic. "Kobayashi," I say slowly. "*Ronin Girl*."

Her face softens and her shoulders relax. She pulls the book out of the stack and looks at it, then at me. "You know Kobayashi?" She has even less of an accent than I do.

"Um, yeah." I relax out of the pose and raise an eyebrow at her, confused. "Why did you pretend not to speak English?"

She does a *you caught me* smile. "It's easier to figure out what people are like if they think you don't understand what they're saying."

I shrug. "I see. What kind of accent do you have?"

"Japanese. What's yours?"

"Polish."

"I like it. You sound like a James Bond villain." She smiles. "I'm Megumi, but a lot of Americans pronounce it Mega Me."

"I'm Maciek Trzebiatowski. Americans call me Chub."

"Yeah, you said that."

My head gets a little warm, but she laughs and it goes away. "So, you're new at Alanmoore?"

She nods. "I went to Trondson last year, but it got shut down, as you know."

I wrinkle my mouth to show her what a shame I think that is. After a short, awkward silence, I go to introduce Moby, but he's gone.

"He . . . disappears sometimes. Don't take it personally."

"I wasn't going to. He looked kinda constipated."

"He's actually the opposite of that."

She laughs. "So how do you even know about *Ronin Girl*?"

"Are you kidding? It's the Holy Grail. Tatsuo Kobayashi is a genius!"

She glances at the book one more time and it almost looks like her eyes roll. "Yeah, he is."

"That's a pretty rare comic to carry around at school."

She looks at the cover. "Yeah, I figured it might help me weed out my kind of people. Looks like it worked." She offers me the book and I'm about to finally lay my hands on it when the bell rings.

"Some other time, I guess." She puts it in her locker and shuts the door as the hall fills with kids. "See you later, Chub." She disappears into the crowd.

I flip my hood over my head like Ben Kenobi disappearing into the crowd in Mos Eisley.

I pass the Boogerloo two more times that afternoon. It stares back at me from where its eyes would be if it wasn't such a hunk of crap.

After school I go straight to Megumi's locker, but she isn't there. I dash to the parking lot to check the bus lines; she's not there either. But Lockhart is, so I duck into the spot behind the Dumpsters to steer clear of her until she's gone.

I press my face between the wall of the school and

the recycling Dumpster so I can watch her supervise the kids getting on the busses, then settle in to wait until the coast is clear.

A voice from the shadows stops me cold. If I had any hair left on my neck it would stand up.

"Still hanging out behind the Dumpsters, huh?" The Arch steps out of the darkest part of the shadows. "I'm just here until she leaves, then it's all yours."

I don't want my voice to crack, so I don't respond.

The instinct to flee is strong, but I stay where I am. His voice is different than it's been the last couple of years. The too-cool tone is missing.

"Did Lockhart get you?" I ask.

He laughs. "Yep."

"She got me too."

"Did she show you the files?"

My head gets hot. "Yeah. She's really on a mission."

"Your file was pretty big." He sounds impressed.

It's the first time in years I've had a conversation with my old friend that wasn't a confrontation. I let myself smile a little. "Well, you kept me pretty busy."

He hangs his head. "I don't play poker anymore."

It's good to know the Cadre's efforts weren't for nothing. "That's good."

He jams his hands in his pockets. "What have you been doing?"

I try to come up with something cool so he doesn't think I've spent the last couple of years obsessing over him. "Tai chi."

"Right, I saw you in the park. Are you still into comics?"

I smile thinking about *Ronin Girl*. "When one catches my eye."

He looks like he's going to say something else, but instead he goes to the crack and peeks out. "Man! She's like the Predator."

We look at each other and at the exact moment say, "Get to the chopper!" in bad Arnold voice. I smile way more than I want to.

When the giggles die out, Arch says, "I got in a lot of trouble from my parents for the uniforms and everything last year."

I never even considered that possibility. "Me too.

My dad almost made me spend the summer in Poland to teach me a lesson."

The Arch's face looks like he just smelled a fart. "That's a little harsh."

"Yeah, you know my parents."

He shakes his head. "I guess they haven't changed." Then he takes a step closer and lowers his voice to a whisper. "Listen, I can't get in trouble again. My parents were talking military school after last year."

"I can't either. I can't handle deportation."

He laughs, then gets serious again. "You know we're the top two names on her list?"

I nod.

"So, what's your plan?"

I don't want to trust him, but it's time to see if he's really changed. "I just have to keep my head down and not give her anything to expel me for."

He nods. "That's pretty much my plan too." He kicks at a flattened juice box with his sneaker. "But what if it doesn't matter? What if she's going to do it to one of us anyway? Do you have a Plan B?"

My head starts to sweat. Since Plan B involves

chucking him under the bus to save my own skin, it's probably best to keep it to myself. "No," I lie.

He lets out a deep breath. "Me either."

I breathe a tiny sigh of relief. But then he continues.

"All I know is if it comes down to it, it's *not* going to be me."

My guts turn to lava. One of the buses revs its engine, ready for one of us to get thrown under its tires. Suddenly I'd rather be anywhere but here.

"I gotta go." I hitch up my pack and step out between the Dumpsters.

Lockhart is lecturing one of the bus drivers about something, with her back to me. While she's distracted I creep along the wall toward the back door of the school. I'll leave through the front door and take the long way around.

Just as I touch the handle she calls, "Mr. Trzebiatowski." But I pretend like I don't hear her and duck through the door.

My footsteps echo in the empty hall, along with the Arch's words. *It's not going to be me.*

If a kid ever needed a Cadre to help him make a plan, now is the time.

Right before the office, I pass the trophy case again. I expect to see the purple glow of the Boogerloo, but it must be switched off for the night. I move closer—to make one last attempt at seeing a kangaroo in the upright puddle of glass—but something is wrong.

The door of the trophy case is open, and the Boogerloo is gone.

CHAPTER 6

I run out the front door of the school, down the steps, and up the sidewalk. There's no way I'm turning around to look until I'm at least two blocks away. A vision of Lockhart chasing me like a liquid metal Terminator makes me ignore my burning lungs until I reach the safety of Mr. Hong's market.

I ask him if I can use the bathroom and he gives me the same suspicious look he always gives me before he says, "Okay, one time!" and jerks his thumb toward the back. I only use his bathroom when I need to ditch someone by crawling out the window into the alley. I wonder if he thinks it's weird that I've gone into that bathroom a lot more times than I've come out of it.

Once I'm in the alley I calm down enough to think. Had I been dumb to believe that the Arch had changed? The only thing that makes sense to me is that he figured it was either him or me, and he'd decided to go with his Plan B before I had a chance to use mine. He must've stolen the Boogerloo while I was distracted looking for Megumi. If he had, it was probably hidden in the shadows the whole time we were talking behind the Dumpsters! Why else would he be lurking back there right after it disappeared?

None of that matters now. The only thing that matters is keeping him from framing me for the heist.

I walk slowly to give my heart a break and to give me time to come up with a plan. But all I can think about is how epically my parents will lose it if I get kicked out of Alanmoore and have to go to school somewhere else. A punishment hasn't been invented yet that will satisfy my dad's thirst for parental vengeance if that happens. But other than exile me to Potatotopia, what's really the worst they can do to me? My stomach spins like an off-balance washing machine when I think the word *homeschool*. I change course and run toward the safest place I can think of. I need to get to the Clairmont Theater.

Visions of what will happen if I get kicked out of Alanmoore whip around in my head. If worse comes to worst, maybe I can become a refugee and seek asylum at Moby's house. Who knows, maybe they'd even adopt me. It'd be kinda cool to have a last name I don't have to spell for people.

My cousin Jarek is in the little glass ticket booth playing around on his phone when I race around the corner in front of the theater. He's never seen me run before, which explains his raised eyebrows. I fling open the door to the lobby, drop my bag, and suck in deep gulps of air.

Jarek comes out of the booth, looking around to make sure no customers are watching. The lobby is empty.

"What's the big hurry, cuz?"

I suck in a few more breaths, then tell him the story, starting with Lockhart threatening me in her office. When I get to the part about the Arch hiding behind the Dumpster, he motions me into the closet he uses for an office.

When I finish, he looks me straight in the eye. "And *you* did not take the booger-man?" he says suspiciously.

"Booger*loo*," I correct him. "And no. I swear it wasn't me."

He strokes the small patch of whiskers he thinks is a goatee. "So what are you going to do?"

"I need some time to make a plan. Can I stay here?"

He nods, then wrinkles his forehead. "What do I say if Uncle Kasmir calls?"

I haven't thought that far ahead. "Just tell him I'm helping you count your Junior Mint inventory or something."

"Will do, dill-doo."

I shake my head. "That's not a thing."

"I'm trying to start a new saying. You don't like it?"

"Never say it again."

He looks hurt but quickly recovers. "You can sit in theater three. No one came to the three o'clock show."

I stand up and thank him. When I turn to go, I spot an old cordless phone on top of the filing cabinet. "Will that phone work in theater three?"

He takes it out of the charger and hands it to me. "Enjoy the show."

Before I settle into the theater, I go to the projection booth and turn the volume all the way down. It's weird watching a movie in a theater with no sound, but it's actually the perfect place to hide out for a few hours. The movie is in black and white, probably part of one of the film festivals the Clairmont is always hosting. On the screen a lady is talking to a guy playing a piano in a bar. I try to read their lips for a minute, but I lose interest when a different guy comes over and starts giving the lady a weepy look. An older teenager whose voice I don't recognize answers the McQueens' phone.

"Yeah?"

"Uhh, is your brother home?"

"Depends. Who's asking?"

"I'm Chub."

"Chub?" There's a pause. "You the bald one the lads won't stop jabbering about?"

The visual of any McQueen "jabbering" makes me pause for a second.

"Yeah, that's me."

"In that case, the runts are here. Which one ya want?"

"Whichever one feels like jabbering," I say.

There's muffled yelling as the older McQueen hollers for one of the triplets to answer the phone. A minute later there's more yelling and then one of the McQueens comes on the line.

"Chub?"

"Yeah. Which—who's this?"

"It's Darwin." I can tell by his tone that he's insulted I can't tell which one I'm talking to.

"Hey Darwin. Listen, it's about school. Things have gotten a little . . ."

". . . Hinky?"

"I guess." He might not talk to me if he knows the Boogerloo was taken, since they'll be suspects too, so I don't mention it. "I think I might need your guys' help with something."

"Yeah, we figured you'd be calling sooner or later."

"You did?"

"We thought you'd ask us to dig something up on old Lockhart for you."

"And?"

He sighs. "Not much. She's pretty clean. We think she's dating the guy who made that preschool project of a mascot."

"Yeah, she already hinted at that." I do my best to hide the desperation in my voice. "So, nothing I can use to get her to back off."

"'Fraid not. We did find out some interesting stuff about some of the new kids at school though."

I'm about to tell him I'm not interested when he says, "You ever heard about a kid they call the Getter?"

Everyone's heard about that kid. Supposedly the Getter can get you anything you need, for a price.

"That's just a legend."

"Well, that legend transferred to Alanmoore when they closed Trondson."

Maybe the Getter can help me put my hands on a certain glass piece of . . . art.

I try to sound uninterested. "What's this kid's name?"

"That depends."

"On what?"

"On whether you still have the magical ability to turn Ds into Bs."

I haven't been to detention yet so I don't know if I can still get access to the librarian, Mrs. Belfry's, computer to change grades, but I'm desperate.

"I can work something out." I hope it's not a lie.

"Good. Do you have a pencil?"

I rifle through my bag and find a pen and paper.

"I'm ready. What's his name?"

The McQueen laughs. "*Her* name is Margot Mercedes."

While I'm writing down the name and the number he says, "We know you'll figure out how to handle Lockhart."

I get a sour taste in my mouth. They shouldn't be relying on me right now. I can't even take care of myself these days.

"I'm working some angles."

"That's our boy." I can almost hear him wink.

I hang up and dial Margot Mercedes's number. The phone picks up on the first ring. The voice is almost too quiet to hear. "Hello."

"Can I speak to Margot, please?"

"Can I say who's calling?"

"No, that's okay." No reason to give out my name if I don't need to.

"I see."

A moment later Margot takes the phone. "Hello?"

I lower my voice to a whisper. "Is this the Getter?"

"Who is this?"

"That's not important right now."

She sounds bored. "The caller ID says the Clairmont Theater. Should I come down there and find you?"

I slap my head and drop the whisper. "No, I go to Alanmoore. I heard you're the person to talk to if I need to . . . acquire something."

Now she lowers her voice. "You heard right. That theater is fifteen minutes away, but I have a bike so I'll be there in five."

I run downstairs and let Jarek know it's okay to let Margot in when she gets there, and on my way back up grab a soda and a bucket of popcorn to munch on. I take my favorite seat in the center of the theater and wait for the Getter to show up.

I'm shoving the first handful of butter-soaked goodness into my mouth when the curtain parts and a little kid walks in. She's dressed like she's going to Sunday school: pigtails and lots of plaid. She looks at the screen, then fixes her eyes on me.

"The bathroom is downstairs." Popcorn shrapnel shoots out of my mouth even though I close my lips.

"Good to know." It's the same voice from the phone.

The McQueens must've made a mistake. "Margot?"

She walks to the end of my row and puts her hands on her hips. "Listen, let's skip the part where you point out that I'm not old enough to go to Alanmoore, so I don't have to point out that you're a bald seventh grader." She raises an eyebrow.

"Um, okay."

"Good." She struts down the aisle toward me.

"Homeschooled until last year. Tested out two years ahead. Voila, fourth grader in middle school." She stops in front of me and points at my head. "What's your story?"

"I got lice and tried to get rid of them with chemicals."

She sucks air through her teeth. "Yikes. I bet you read warning labels now."

I make a one-note laugh. Even though the theater is as cold as a meat locker my head starts to sweat, so I change the subject. "How'd you become a Getter?"

Her hands go back to her hips. "Actually, I'm *the* Getter. The difference is small but significant."

I volley her joke back at her. "Like you."

At first she's not amused, then she smiles. "Yeah, I like that." She sits next to me. "I'm really good at getting what I want. Older kids are nicer when I help them out. Voila, I became the Getter. You do what you gotta do to fit in. You know how it is."

I consider telling her I've never really tried to fit in, but then change my mind.

She grunts as she lifts an oversize purse onto her

lap. "You want some Junior Mints for that corn?"

I shake my head.

She shrugs. "Suit yourself." She rips the top off the box and stuffs a few in her mouth, followed by a handful of popcorn.

"So, what is it you need got?" she asks.

I try to think of a way to say it without raising any red flags. I draw a complete blank.

"This is confidential, right?"

She holds up her palms. "Of course."

Before I can chicken out I blurt, "I need a genuine Wahoolie Electric Kangaroo, and I need it quick."

She pops another handful of mints in her mouth. "That's easy. There's one in the trophy case at school." She dusts off her hands and closes her bag to go.

I lower my voice for effect. "No, there isn't."

She looks at me, confused, then realization spreads across her face. "Somebody stole the Boogerloo?"

I look around as though someone may have heard. "Yeah."

"When? I saw it today."

"Sometime this afternoon."

Judging by the look on her face, the gears in her head are spinning. She squints and gives me a suspicious look. "Why do you want it?"

"I have my reasons." I don't want her to know how much I need it and drive the price up. "Let's just say it's very important that it gets got."

"You don't strike me as an art collector. Are you into mascots?"

"Something like that."

"You shoulda called yesterday. I just sold a slightly used kangaroo costume. It had this weird stain, but the buyer didn't mind."

Last year Moby stained the arm of the school's old mascot costume with purple Gatorade while improvising during a plot. Margot must've found it after the custodian, Mr. Kraley, threw it out. I can't help wrinkling my nose remembering how bad the inside of the mascot costume smelled. "Who the heck would want that?"

She makes a *tsking* noise and wags a finger.

"Right, confidential."

She stands up suddenly and she's barely taller than

I am sitting down. She shoves the rest of the mints into my hand. "I'll be in touch if I come up with anything."

I jump to my feet. "So that's it."

"I need to go. I have another appointment." She skips down the row and out of the theater.

Telling her what I'm looking for was a mistake. Something like that is worth way more than I'd ever be able to pay for it. And what was the deal with her suddenly remembering another appointment?

She's one of a very few people who know the thing is missing, and she's on her way to some sort of mystery appointment. For all I know *she* might've stolen it. I need to follow her and see what's up.

I shout good-bye and thanks to Jarek as I sprint out the door. I look both ways, then run to the corner and look up a side street before I spot her pedaling away. There's no way I can keep up with her on her bike. I'll have to guess where she's going and pray that I'm right.

Where would I arrange a secret meeting with someone? I'd pick a spot where a kid wouldn't look out of place.

Suddenly, I know where I would go if I were her.

Instead of following her, I cut through an alley I used several times last summer as a shortcut to the park where I practice tai chi.

I quickly find the hole in the fence where the chain-link part isn't attached to the post and slide through. Then I dash under the cover of a giant willow tree across from the main playground. Deep in the tree's shadow is the perfect spot to watch the rest of the park. A quick scan tells me she isn't there. I'm about to call it a bad hunch and head for Moby's house when I spot her pedaling her blue one-speed up the path. She stops at the climbing castle at the center of the playground, flips out the kickstand, and casually strolls over to a bench and sits.

I look around to see if anyone is walking toward her, but she is just sitting on the bench alone.

"What is your deal, kid?" I whisper under my breath. Then I notice her lips are moving. She's talking, but there's no one on the bench with her. I'm about to declare her crazy when she stands up suddenly, just like she had with me. When she walks away, the person sitting on the bench behind hers with their back to her stands up to walk away too.

I'd recognize that luxurious mop of hair anywhere. But what I need to know is if the Arch is here to buy or to sell.

CHAPTER 7

I get home before my parents and fake a stomachache to get out of dinner. It also builds a little presympathy in case Lockhart calls and blames me for the theft. It really sells my story when I fall asleep at seven thirty out of pure mental exhaustion.

The fact that I wake up alive the next morning means Lockhart must not have called. I throw on clothes and race out of the house before my parents wake up. I need to get to school early and search for the Boogerloo. Plus, I don't want to look guilty by not showing up the day after it disappeared.

With nobody to talk to, I have plenty of time to think. Who would even want that thing enough to steal it? No matter what scenario I imagine, I end up in the same place every time. It's probably not even about the Boogerloo; it's about needling Lockhart and in the process maybe getting her to expel someone you only pretend to like. A vision of the Arch's cocky grin flashes in my mind. If he did steal it, and manages to pin it on me, it'll be sweet revenge for ruining his poker career last year.

Then another thought occurs to me. What if it wasn't him? Lockhart put the heat on a bunch of students, not just the two of us. Is it possible he's just as desperate to clear his name as I am?

I'm guessing at a list of possible suspects when I trip over something and face-plant on the sidewalk.

"Dude!" a voice says behind me.

I hop up, dust my jeans off, then look back.

Megumi crawls out of the hedge that runs down the side of the school and looks me up and down. "Are you okay?"

"I think I'll live," I say. But based on the vicious

case of pins and needles in my wrists, I'm not entirely sure I will.

She squats down and gathers up the papers that tumbled out of my bag when I fell, then hands them back to me with a smile. "Sorry. I guess my feet were sticking out." She nods toward the hedge. "It's a good place to read."

"There's a nice spot behind the Dumpsters," I offer. "It smells really bad, but you get used to it."

She wrinkles her nose. "I like the hedge. It's not as . . ."

". . . Garbage-y?" I start to sweat, suddenly aware I just admitted that I like to hang out behind a Dumpster.

"Exactly."

A tiny pebble is stuck in the scrape on my hand. I pick it out and flick it away. Her forehead wrinkles in a nervous look.

"It doesn't hurt," I lie.

Her face softens. "I'm really sorry."

I don't want her to feel bad so I change the subject. "Why are you here so early?"

"My stepmother is a horrible cook so I leave early when my dad is out of town."

I laugh. "How horrible?"

"On the first day of school she made me a bowl of crushed-up ramen with milk poured on it. I think she thought it was Japanese cereal."

"My mom makes headcheese and eggs."

"What's headcheese?"

I shake my head. "You don't want to know. But it's worse than it sounds."

Megumi laughs, then kicks a bark chip back under the hedge.

"Is your dad gone a lot?" I ask.

"Yeah. It's for work."

"I wish my parents would get jobs like that."

This time she doesn't laugh; in fact, her smile disappears completely. I make a mental note to not bring that up again.

Then it's her turn to change the subject. "Why are *you* here so early? Headcheese again?"

I want to say it's because my parents don't travel

enough, but I don't want to make her feel bad. "I have to find something before school."

She nods and we stand in silence for a minute. I want to read *Ronin Girl* more than anything, but there's something else about her that makes me want to hang out with her. Just walking away doesn't feel right. "Want to talk about comics at lunch?"

She pushes out her lower lip. "I guess."

She raises and lowers her shoulders and then walks past me toward the front door. When she's a few feet away she stops and turns around. "I'll see you at lunch."

I hope so.

I go around to the back of the school by the parking lot and sneak in through a side door. I take the back stairs to avoid Lockhart. If she wants me, she'll have to come find me.

As kids fill the halls I head to the main staircase and walk down to the landing between the first and second floors. The trophy case is at the bottom of the stairs, so the landing is the best place to see it without being spotted from the principal's office.

Half of me stupidly expects it to be there, that maybe Lockhart had it in her office to polish it or something. I hold onto that hope until I hit the landing, squat down, and see that it's still gone.

A steady stream of kids floods past the case now. None of them seem to notice that our mascot is missing. *So much for school pride.* Then as I'm about to walk away, the Arch makes a slow cruise past the case. He turns his head slightly toward the empty shelf as he passes, then disappears down the hallway. *He's returning to the scene of the crime.*

I slink down the stairs and blend into the river of kids in the hall. The Arch is taller than everyone so it's easy to follow him. I tail him to his locker but hang back in the alcove at the top of the stairs. From here I'll be able to see into his locker when he opens it. If he's stupid enough to hide it in there, I'll have him.

When he's about to open his locker something catches his eye and he turns. I have to lean around the corner to see. It's Megumi, and she's all smiles. I'm so focused on the two of them that I don't even notice that most of the kids have disappeared from the hall. I only have a second to wonder why before Lockhart scissor-walks into view. The Arch's back is turned so Megumi sees her first. Moby could take notes on the disappearing act that Ronin Girl pulls.

Lockhart says something to the Arch and his shoulders sag. She turns to go and he follows behind her like a puppy that just pooped on the rug.

Just as I'm about to go, a hand lands on my shoulder. The shriek I make sounds like the brakes on my dad's car.

Shelby takes her hand off my shoulder and pats her chest like an old lady trying to calm down. "Wow! That didn't make you look guilty or anything."

I wipe my head and straighten up. "Why are you sneaking up on me, Shelby?"

She stabs her nose toward the Arch's locker. "It looks like you're the one doing the sneaking."

"I was . . ." No excuse comes to me.

She pushes her glasses up and folds her arms. "Uh-huh, that's what I thought. So were you planning on including any of us in this little plot of yours?"

"What plot?"

She tilts her head to one side. "Really? Who else would take the Electric Kangaroo out of the trophy case?"

I give her my most serious look. "It wasn't me. I think the Arch is trying to frame me."

Her face softens. "Why do you think that?"

I tell her about the conversation behind the Dumpster, then his meeting with Margot.

She thinks about it for second. "Well, with your reputation you're a pretty easy guy to frame."

My head gets hot.

Her look switches from accusatory to concerned. "What's the plan?"

"I don't know. Find it, I guess. She just hauled the Arch into her office. She'll probably put the school on lockdown and then bring me in and sweat me."

The first bell rings and I flinch again like a nervous cat. "I just think we should keep it quiet. We don't want anyone to hear us talking about it before it even goes public, okay?"

Shelby nods and we walk to class together. Sizzler

has seats saved for us. He pulls his backpack off the one closest to his and offers it to Shelby.

Moby stumbles into homeroom and scans the room looking for us. Shelby and I look like a pterodactyl and her egg sitting there; we can't be that hard to spot.

He hurries over. "Chub, the Boogerloo is gone, just like you said!"

I try unsuccessfully to turtle my head into my neck, then peer around to see if anyone heard him. Thankfully, nobody turns to look.

I put a finger to my lips. "Shhhhh."

"Why?" he says in his horrible whisper. "I thought you wanted someone to steal it to teach Lockhart—"

I lunge out of my desk and clamp my hand over his mouth. Thankfully, the bell rings, and Mrs. Badalucco comes in to start the class. She flops into her chair and starts mopping her chins with a wad of napkins from her desk drawer. She's almost dry when the intercom crackles.

Commence lockdown in three . . . two . . .

"This is Principal Lockhart. The cafeteria floor will be waxed this weekend, so please stack your chairs neatly when you are finished with lunch on Friday. That is all." The intercom snaps off with a click.

Mrs. Badalucco flips a goofy salute at the speaker, which gets a nervous laugh from the class.

Shelby raises her eyebrows and mimes wiping sweat off her forehead. But I'm not ready to wipe mine just yet.

Mrs. B is clearing her throat to start class when there's a knock on the door and Mrs. Osborne scurries into the room. She hands Mrs. B a piece of paper, then slips out of the room without making eye contact.

I already know what the paper says, so I start putting my books back in my bag.

The wet clump of neck napkins makes a gong sound as Mrs. Badalucco tosses it in the empty trash can. Then she holds up the sheet of paper. "Alphabet Soup-ski, you're up."

Apparently my "good guy" status with Mrs. Osborne has expired, because she won't look me in the eye when I walk into the office. I don't even make it to the waiting bench before Lockhart's voice seeps out of her office.

"Come in, Mr. Trzebiatowski. This will only take a moment."

This time Lockhart already has a cup of tea made. Her gray, snake-like eyes watch me over the rim of the mug. I take my usual seat across from her and try to look as casual as possible despite the fact it feels like there are two porcupines wrestling in my guts.

After a few noisy slurps and a loud "Ahhhh," she sets down the mug.

"Is there anything you'd like to tell me?"

A few things come to mind, but if I say any of them to her face it will only make the situation worse.

"Nope." I make a little popping sound on the *P* and look her straight in the eyes. Her left one twitches slightly.

"Then I'll make this short and sweet." She leans forward on her elbows. "I will find out who took the Wahoolie, and when I do," she pauses and breathes in deeply, "that person will be expelled."

This isn't fair. Sure, I joked about stealing it—

maybe even wanted to—but I didn't. My head starts to bead up. Not from nervousness; this time I'm angry.

"Does that upset you, Mr. Trzebiatowski?"

I don't talk until I'm sure my voice won't waver. "I. Didn't. Take. It."

She smiles as though I've just walked into a trap. "I saw you sneak into the school right before it disappeared."

"That doesn't prove anything. There were other kids here yesterday too."

"And they will all have a chance to come clean, just as I'm giving you. As I said, I will find out who the thief is." Her smile spreads. "Don't worry. I have plenty of suspects."

I sit back in my chair. "What if you never find out who took it? What are you going to do, expel all of us?"

She sits back in her chair and steeples her fingers. "If I don't find out which one of you stole it, that's exactly what I'm going to do."

CHAPTER 8

Since there's no way to prove I'm not the thief, and since Lockhart has files as thick as dictionaries on all her suspects, there's only one way out of this mess. I have to find the stupid thing, no matter what.

I don't feel like going back to class right away, so I take the long way through the halls and stop by my locker to grab books for my next class. When I open the door a piece of paper falls to the floor by my feet. At first it looks like trash and I almost toss it in the bin, but instead I unfold it and read.

Meet me at the last place we talked.

Lunch

—A

The last place we talked was behind the Dumpsters.

The last time he and I needed to get ourselves out of trouble, we tried to kill our head lice with some chemicals from my dad's shop, and I ended up bald. Without thinking about it, I rub my hand over my head. It's as smooth as a bowling ball. Even though I don't want to meet the Arch in a dark corner, I know what I have to do. I'm going to hear what he has to say, because this game of stolen Boogerloos and possible expulsion is just like my hair: I have nothing left to lose.

The rest of the morning passes more slowly than the week before Christmas. Even the kids who would've teased me in the halls last year make an extra effort to avoid me. Lockhart has managed to suck the spirit out of the school in less than a week.

When the bell rings for lunch my stomach flops. Megumi is waiting for me in the lunchroom with a copy of *Ronin Girl*, but if I don't sort things out with the Arch I might never get to read another comic again in my life. There's only one choice that makes sense right now. I race down the stairs to get to the Dumpsters first. I need to be there before him to make sure he isn't setting up some sort of a trap. I bump into the McQueens on the stairs. None of them has a hat so they don't say a word, but judging by their narrowed eyes and sly smiles, they've figured out why I called them last night.

It can't hurt to have a little security and maybe a few witnesses in case the Arch tries to pull something, so I give them the short version.

"I didn't take the Boogerloo, but I need to find it or lots of kids are going to pay. The Arch is a suspect too and he wants to talk."

They scowl when I mention my old nemesis.

"I don't have time to negotiate. So if you guys make sure I'm not about to get my doopah kicked in, I'll make it worth your while." With a quick three-way glance, the decision is made. They follow me down the stairs and post up in the parking lot as inconspicuously as possible for three people with hair like lit road flares.

I don't have to press myself into the shadows behind the Dumpster for long. The Arch strolls in a moment later. He flips down the hood of his sweatshirt and smooths his hand over his hair. The move makes an old hurt in my stomach flinch like a zombie waking up. He probably doesn't mean for it to. But maybe he does. Before his eyes have time to adjust to the darkness, I slide out of the shadows. His tiny flinch when he sees me makes me smile. "I guess you got the note."

I hold up the paper. "What's this about?"

He throws up his hands. "Seriously? Lockhart is on a seek-and-destroy mission."

"And?"

He drops his hands to his side. "And *what*? We can't let her do this to us."

The word "*us*" makes the zombie in my guts claw itself out of its grave.

"She talked to you too, didn't she?" he demands.

I nod.

"I don't know what she said to you," he says. "But

she told me she'd get rid of as many students as it takes to get the kid who stole it."

"So why don't you just return it and we can go back to business as usual?"

"Very funny. I didn't take it." There's no trace of the cocky, cool *the Arch* tone in his voice.

My hand wants to go to my head, but I force it to stay at my side. I don't want him to know I'm nervous. "What do you mean 'we can't let her do this to us'? Yesterday all you cared about was that it wasn't you."

He holds up the palms of his hands again. "Have you been paying attention? She's crazy, and now she's angry. She doesn't care who she has to take out to retaliate for this. That means we're in this together."

Assuming he's telling the truth and he's not the thief, he has a point. Like it or not, we both need to find the thing.

Then a thought hits me. "Why are you even a suspect? You're the class president."

A real smile, not an Arch smirk, crosses his lips.

"Well, you might not know this, but I did almost burn down the school last year."

The comment floats in the air for a moment before I crack a smile of my own.

"Yeah, you did."

He shrugs. "Hey, I was young and stupid."

We laugh together, and for the moment my stomach-zombie slumps back into the hole he crawled out of.

"So, what, you called me here to try and team up?"

He shoves his chin out and widens his eyes. "Who else knows how to sneak around this place better than us?"

I raise my eyebrow and let the question hang.

"Plus you've got all of your—you know, your gang or whatever."

"Cadre," I correct him.

"Right."

There's a flat juice box on the ground that looks like it's been digested by a hippo. I shove it around with the toe of my shoe.

"What about your gang?" I say, remembering how

Nate and Marlon kidnapped me the last time the Arch wanted to call a truce.

He laughs. "Those guys couldn't plot their way through a trapdoor if it opened under their feet."

The visual of those two goons falling into a dungeon of fire gives me an odd feeling of warmth. "I thought they were your friends."

"We hang out together, but since last year they've been . . . different."

I know the look on his face when his chin sinks. I've felt it before.

"So you're asking me to trust you."

He shoves his hands in his pockets and kicks at the digested juice box. "I'm saying *we* need to trust *each other* unless we both want to end up in military school or something."

I wish he wasn't right, but it really is as simple as that. I need to get out of here and talk to the Cadre. "Let me think it over."

"We don't have time for that. What do I need to do to convince you?"

"The Cadre has certain—capabilities," I say. "But what do you bring to the table?"

He shifts on his feet. He has something but he's not sure if he wants to tell me yet.

I tap my bare wrist. "Tick-tock."

After a short staring contest, he rolls his shoulders and sighs. "Okay, Lockhart has a camera."

This is a surprise but I try not to show it. "Where?"

"In the hall, aimed at the trophy case."

"I've never seen it."

He gives me a look like I just said something dumb. "I'm the tallest kid at Alanmoore. Trust me, it's there."

"Wait, if she has a camera, that means she knows it wasn't either of us."

"That's what I'm saying. But if she knows who did it, why's she putting us through all this?"

Something scrapes on the brick on the other side of the Dumpster. It might be a kid, but it might be Lockhart.

"We need to see that footage from yesterday."

The Arch taps his nose with his finger. "Bingo."

"What do you think, I have access to her computer?"

"You just said you guys have capabilities."

I don't want him knowing exactly what we're capable of. "Yeah, but—"

He catches my eyes with his. "Do you think I didn't notice a mysterious drop in my grades last year? I don't know how you did it, but I know it was you."

I hope it's dark enough that he can't see me go red. I bob my head as though I'm trying to decide, but the tip on the camera is too important to ignore. Besides, if the footage shows the Arch is the thief, why would he tell me about it?

"So, are we in business?" He raises his fist toward me and I jump back out of pure instinct. He looks at his fist and laughs.

I feel pretty stupid when I realize he's offering me his version of a handshake to seal our deal. I haven't done many fist bumps, so my technique isn't good. A combination of nerves and adrenaline makes me crash my fist into his, sending an explosion of pain up my arm.

He pulls back and rubs the sting out of his hand. "Well, that was weird."

"Sorry," I say. "I'm out of practice."

"You'll get used to it." He shoves his hand in his pocket. "So, does that mean I'm in?"

Did the Arch just ask to join the Cadre?

"In what?"

"Your Cadre."

Something like nervousness on steroids hits me and my head swims. If you asked me which was more likely, Moby pooping out an armadillo that could work a yo-yo, or the Arch asking to join the Cadre, I would've put my entire comic book collection on the armadillo.

I have no idea how to answer him, so I do the only thing I can. I mumble, "We'll be in touch," and then get out of there as fast as I can.

CHAPTER 9

When I emerge from behind the Dumpster, I throw a thumbs-up to the first McQueen I see. He nods, signals his brothers, and leaves to scarf down his lunch in whatever time is left. To my right, I hear the scraping sound again. I look over and Moby is rubbing his riveted pockets against the bricks.

"What are you doing?"

He stops rubbing and walks toward me. "I was looking for you."

I meant the *polishing the school with his butt* thing, but I probably don't want to hear his answer, so I let it go.

"What were you doing behind the Dumpster?"

"Figuring out a way to catch the real thief." Every member of the Cadre has good reasons not to trust the Arch, so I'm not going to tell them we're talking until I absolutely have to. I hustle him toward the cafeteria before he sees the Arch come out from behind the Dumpster.

"Did you figure it out?"

"Not exactly, but I think at least I know how to prove it wasn't me."

Moby nods the way he does when he is only pretending to understand. "You figured that out behind the Dumpster?"

"I was actually meeting someone who wants to join the Cadre."

Moby's shoulders slump. "Who?"

After his freak-out when Shelby joined last year, I have to be careful. "You wouldn't believe me if I told you."

"Why? Is it the Arch?"

My throat makes a weird swallowing noise I can't control. I try to laugh it off, but my voice comes out four octaves higher than normal. "What?"

"I dunno. You said I wouldn't believe it, so . . ."

The deafening clang of the bell scares us both and sidetracks the conversation.

"Listen, Mobe. There's a camera."

He looks around nervously. "Where?"

"Not here. Lockhart put a camera in the main hall. A—someone told me about it. It's pointed at the Boogerloo." I pause for him to do the math on his own.

He tries to snap his fingers, but they make no sound. "We need to see what's on the camera so we know who the thief is."

"Exactly," I say, relieved his mind is no longer on whoever might be joining the Cadre.

"How are we going to do that?"

"I need to get on Mrs. Belfry's laptop. I bet if I can get back into the school's main system I can get to the camera."

"But you only go to the library for detention. And if you get a detention, Lockhart won't—"

I cut him off with a hand on his shoulder. "I'm gonna have to get in there a different way."

"How?"

I look him in the eye. "It's just like the Colonel always says."

"'Don't put the spoon back in the mayonnaise after you licked it'?"

"What? No!" I force back a bit of puke that rises in my throat. "'If you want to dance . . .'" I leave it for Moby to finish.

He points at me when he has it. "'. . . You gotta pay the guy with the accordion!'"

"Exactly."

"What are we waiting for? Let's go break into the music room before lunch is over!"

"No, Mobe. I didn't mean that literally."

He looks disappointed. "You aren't making any sense, Chub."

"What I mean is, you are looking at Alanmoore's new library volunteer."

At the final bell I fight the river of kids going down the stairs and make my way up to the library. Mrs. Belfry's been busy since last year. Construction paper leaves are taped up all over the place and there's even a small scarecrow sitting on a bale of hay right by the main door. I don't remember her ever putting up decorations before, but I guess if you have to pick up a hobby during your second century, cutting up construction paper is probably pretty safe.

The place looks abandoned. That is, until Moby flies through the door a second later.

"Am I late?" he says loudly enough to be heard over a jet engine.

I put a finger to my lips and shake my head. "Just talk normally," I say, knowing it will be quieter than if he tries to whisper.

He straightens up. "Oh good, whispering is exhausting. Did you talk to her yet?"

"No, I—"

"Who's there?" Mrs. Belfry calls from the back office.

"Hi, Mrs. Belfry. It's Chub," I call back. Then I turn to Moby. "Just let me do the talking."

He gives me a thumbs-up and we stroll to her office.

She's almost hidden behind all the cat figurines and pictures cramming her desk. She pokes her head above the clutter looking like she just woke up. "Chub?"

I wave from the doorway. "Hi, remember me?"

She pats her head searching for her glasses, then realizes she already has them on. She peers at me over the top of the frames. "Are you a student?"

Great. I'm going to have to rebuild all the trust I built last year to be able to trick her into letting me on her computer again. "I helped you with your computer last year during detention."

She studies me for a moment, then something clicks. "Maciek Trzebiatowski. You updated my Tardis driver and cured the Dalek virus for me last year!"

Moby giggles and I have to force myself not to.

"Yep, that was me."

Her smile fades as quickly as it came, and she clasps her hands together over her heart. "Did you get detention already, dear?"

"No, no. I just figured you might want someone to have a look at your computer and—"

"He's here to volunteer," Moby says before I can finish.

Then the smile is back on her face. "Volunteer? How wonderful!"

Faster than I thought possible she jumps out of her seat, grabs my hand, and pats it. "Just wonderful."

I move toward the computer on her desk. "So I guess I'll just see . . ." But she doesn't let go of my hand. I try to pull away, but she has superhuman old-lady strength, probably from scooping out a hundred litter boxes a night.

She shakes her head. "Oh, I don't need you to do that."

I shoot a nervous glance at Moby, then look up into her folded leather face. "You don't?" I stop trying to pull away and she lets go of my hand.

"That's what I have Kyle for."

A vision flashes to mind of one of her cats tapping away at her keyboard. Moby raises his eyebrows and twirls his finger around his ear in the universal sign for "crazy."

"Kyle? Who's Kyle?"

Then there's another voice from the closet in the back of her office. "Did someone say my name?"

The person who must be Kyle emerges holding a stack of books. He's about Jarek's age, but that's where the similarities end. Jarek always looks like he woke up three minutes before you saw him. Kyle looks like he just came from a photo shoot for a clothing catalog. He sets down the books and walks over to me.

Mrs. Belfry beams. "Kyle, this is Maciek."

Kyle extends his hand and I shake it.

"Maciek. Polish, right?"

I narrow my eyes, waiting for the inevitable joke, but he doesn't make it.

"Right."

This is going bad quickly. It's time for what the Colonel calls a "tactical retreat."

I jerk my thumb at the door. "I was just—"

Mrs. Belfry interrupts. "He came to volunteer!"

Kyle is impressed. "Neat-o! I'm brand spanking new to student teaching, so I can use all the help I can get. I've got another shopping bag full of leaves to put up."

Forget retreat, I need to escape. "Actually . . ."

But before I can finish Kyle picks up the stack of books and dumps them in my arms. "Let's start by introducing you to your new best friend, Dewey."

If Dewey is anything like Kyle, I will have to jump out the window and figure out the rest of the plan during the four-story plummet to the ground. This is what I get for rushing in without planning. At least I'll have Moby here to serve my self-inflicted sentence with me.

"We don't really know how to . . . library," I say, hoping to throw the brakes on Kyle's enthusiasm.

Kyle chuckles and gives me a questioning look. "Who's we?"

I spin to nod at Moby, but he's nowhere to be seen.

My first half hour with Kyle is a working lecture on the Dewey decimal system, followed by an aerobic reorganization of the encyclopedia shelf. After forty-five minutes that feel like about 127 hours, Kyle takes a break from talking to run to the bathroom.

This is my chance.

I figure I have three minutes at the most to get on

the computer before he returns and starts in again. As soon as the library door creaks shut I dash to Mrs. Belfry's office. She's sound asleep in her chair, but there's enough room for me to get at the computer if she doesn't move.

I open the Admin icon and type as quietly as possible.

Username: IrmaBelfry

Password: MRDARCY

I do a tiny fist pump when the welcome screen comes up. I scroll through the entire menu, but there's nothing about cameras or surveillance.

I minimize the window and scan her desktop for the link to the security system. There isn't one. The clock on the wall ticks away. I have maybe thirty seconds before Kyle comes back and I have some explaining to do.

I open the Finder and type *Camera*.

No results.

I'm punching in *Surveillance* when the main door of the library creaks open. Kyle's footsteps pad across the carpet toward the office.

"C'mon," I beg the machine through gritted teeth.

The chasing circle completes one more loop, then a blank box appears on the screen. Belfry's machine is a dead end. I flick my fingers over the trackpad, closing all the windows, finally hitting the X on the Admin window just as Kyle rounds the corner.

He pats his stomach. "You know what they say, you don't buy green tea, you rent it."

I jump to attention, then try to look as casual as possible.

Kyle narrows his eyes. "What are you doing?"

I try to think of a good reason, any reason, why I'd be on the laptop when Mrs. Belfry lets out a snore like a bantha with a sinus infection.

I point at the computer. "It was beeping so I muted it."

Kyle's eyes stay narrow. Then Mrs. Belfry snorts again and his face softens.

"Poor thing. I guess she really needs a nap." He laughs and I quickly laugh too so he doesn't ask any more questions.

Fifteen minutes later I say good-bye to him and

race down the stairs. The camera thing had sounded too good to be true when the Arch told me about it. I'm not surprised I didn't find anything.

I'm almost to the first floor when something occurs to me: I've never actually *seen* this camera. I only have the Arch's word it actually exists. When I get to the landing between floors I crouch down and look down the stairs toward the first-floor hallway. From this angle I can see most of the trophy case, but my view of the top of it is blocked by the second-floor landing above. I walk down a few steps, careful not to go too far and get caught on camera sneaking around the halls after hours. When I get far enough down the stairs that the whole trophy case is visible, I'm too low to see if there's anything on top.

I need a higher angle with nothing blocking the view. A quick glance around tells me what I have to do. If I can balance myself between the railings of the two staircases I'll be able to see what I need to see.

I strain against my jeans and barely get my foot up on the railing, then grab the railing pointing up to the second floor and pull myself up. I have to put one foot on the up railing and one on the down to be able to balance. When I look down at the first floor, half a story below, my vision narrows. Suddenly my heartbeat in my ears sounds like Moby's legs rubbing together in a pair of corduroys. Apparently, I'm afraid of heights.

I inch my way down the railing. When I get to the point where I can't stretch any farther I still can't see the top of the case. But if I can just move one foot a tiny bit closer, I know I'll be able to see the top clearly from this angle.

I summon all my tai chi training and breathe deeply as I stretch. My jeans do not have any martial arts train-ing, but they decide to suck in a deep breath too. Cool air rushes in as the crotch of my pants splits wide open. I don't know which is worse: focusing on not becoming a real-life Humpty Dumpty, or the prospect of some-one walking under me and looking up. But this is a matter of life and death, and I'm almost there.

I push myself a little farther, finally getting an unblocked view of the top of the trophy case. Other than a couple of inches of dust, it is completely bare.

The Arch sent me on a wild-goose chase.

I'm about to figure out how to get down when something occurs to me. The Arch said it was pointed *at* the case. That means it's on the other side of the hall.

Still gripping the upper railing for dear life, I crouch down to look at the other side of the hall. Next to the door to the office, facing the trophy case, is another cabinet, the one Mrs. Osborne decorates for different seasons and where the theater club advertises their latest production.

Then my seventh worst fear comes true.

The door directly below me opens with a jerk. I don't have to look down to know who it is. There's no mistaking the metal clack of Lockhart's heels on the floor.

I have no choice but to freeze and pray.

As the footsteps pass below me I force my eyes down. Her flattop passes just below my left foot on the lower railing. She's almost in her office, and I'm about to let out the breath I'm holding in, when she suddenly stops.

No amount of aerobic library reorganization training can prepare you for holding in a breath and a nervous fart, while straddling an abyss, with a huge hole in the crotch of your pants while your pit bull principal stands below you.

I'm about to yell "I give up" or just let the fart go, when she walks to the trophy case. Her reflection is crystal clear in the glass. She stands there for a moment, probably tearing up over her precious Wahoolie. She straightens her blazer and turns to go, but then something stops her. She turns slowly and returns to where she was. She leans in, trying to see something in the glass.

This is it. Game over.

But instead of whipping around and catching me doing my impression of a chandelier, she breathes on the glass, and then polishes the spot with the cuff of her blazer. Then she does a quick nod of approval and disappears into her office.

I wait for the sound of her door closing before I breathe. I let go of the upper railing and put my hand on the wall so I can slide down enough to see the top of the cabinet. Just like the Arch said, there's a small webcam up there pointed straight at the spot where the Boogerloo used to be.

As gracefully as a drunk gymnast, I dismount the railing and take a deep breath. When my knees stop shaking I slink down the stairs, careful to stay in the camera's blind spot. There are no wires coming off the camera. A trap door opens in my guts when I realize why I couldn't bring it up on Belfry's machine. It isn't wired into the school's system. The camera probably records directly onto Lockhart's personal computer in her office.

If I want to see what's on that video, that's where I have to go too.

CHAPTER 10

After slinking home with my coat tied around my waist and changing my pants, I head over to Moby's. The Colonel whips the door open like he's surprising a machine gun nest full of enemy soldiers. I make the mistake of looking over his outfit, then say a prayer that I'm not around when that badly stressed seam on his boxers finally lets go.

He quickly scans the street, then waves me inside. "Who pooped in your mess kit?"

I drop my bag and take off my shoes. "It's a long story, sir."

The Colonel wrinkles his forehead. "It doesn't involve crying or soccer or anything, does it?"

I assure him it doesn't.

"All right. *Extreme Alaskan Llama Ranchers* is on at sixteen thirty hours." He looks at his watch. "You've got twelve minutes. Step into my office."

The Colonel's "office" is actually the Dicks' theater room. Moby is in there playing video games when we walk in.

He glances at me, but keeps playing. "Hey, Chub. How was the library?"

I throw my hands up. "Oh, it was great. Thanks for asking."

"Did you get on the computer?"

"Just for a second when Kyle went to the bathroom."

"Well?"

"Nothing there. Then Kyle made me move the encyclopedias to the other side of the library. Did you know they still had those?"

Moby makes a sour face and pauses his game. "That guy was scary."

I take the chair next to the Colonel and flip out my footrest.

The Colonel shakes his head and laughs. "What do you need a computer for? You just said they have encyclopedias."

Moby rolls his eyes. "It's not the same thing, Grandpa."

"Horse apples! Where do you think they found all the stuff they put on the Internet?"

I need just the right approach if I want him to help. "Sir, I have a question for you. It's about tactics."

The redness goes out of his face, replaced by a sly grin. "Tactics is my middle name. What have you got?"

On the way over, I came up with a way to grill him without letting him know what's really going on. "Well, there's this big capture the flag tournament and it's really important that we win. But the other team has one player who's amazing at defense."

He nods. "I assume this kid is faster and more athletic than you?"

"Well, yeah," I say.

"Makes sense. So even if you capture their flag, you probably won't make it back without being caught."

"Exactly."

The Colonel rubs his steel-wool stubble. "This calls for the old honey pot. Reminds me of this one time back in seventy—I don't want to get too specific. This terrorist stole a bunch of missile launch codes and threatened to use them if we came after him."

Here we go. I give Moby a slight chin-raise. He tries to do it back but he just looks like he got rear ended in a bumper car.

"Anyway, intel told us he had a thing for this actress, Valerie something."

"A *thing*, sir?"

"He was obsessed with her. As far as we could tell she was the only thing he cared about, other than money, so we floated a story that she was in the same city we knew he was hiding out in. We made sure he knew she'd be at the disco at ten one night."

I sit forward in my chair. "Did he go for it?"

"Like a fly to honey."

Moby looks concerned. "How did you get her to go along with it?"

"She wasn't there. He just needed to think she was long enough to let his guard down and let us capture his flag. He sent one of his bodyguards to scope it out. The bodyguard led us right back to where he was holed up. The rest is all gunshots and swear words. What you need to do is figure out who this other player's Valerie is."

He's right; a plugged toilet won't cut it with Lockhart. We need her to take herself out of the game long enough for me to get on her computer. And lucky for me, I think I know just who her Valerie is.

I spend most of the weekend at Moby's house, which is nice for two reasons: I can plan out Monday's operation without my parents looming over me, and it gets me out of having to sort *the pile* at my parents' shop for at least a week. Before I go back to my house Sunday afternoon I use the Dicks' phone to make sure everybody is ready for the next day. When Moby gets that look in his eye and excuses himself to go to the bathroom, I make the final call, the one I don't want to make in front of him.

"Hello," the Arch says over the sound of a very loud TV in the background.

"It's Chub."

There's a rustling noise, then the sound in the background is gone. "Sorry, I was watching the game with my dad. I'm in a different room now. How did it go? Did you see the video?"

"I couldn't get it. The camera is linked directly to Lockhart's computer."

He sighs on the other end of the line. "So, what now?"

My heartbeat drums in my chest. I can't believe I'm saying this to the Arch. "I came up with a plan."

"To get on Lockhart's personal laptop? Are you nuts?"

"Do you know another way to get our hands on it?"

Arch pauses again. "No. So, what's your plan?"

"Not my plan," I correct him. "*Our* plan."

"So, now you want me in the group?" There's a trace of cockiness in his tone I don't like.

"Do you want to help or not?"

"Yeah, I'm in."

Down the hall the toilet flushes.

"I gotta go. Meet us behind the Dumpsters tomorrow morning. Shelby will get you set up."

His answer is cut off by me hanging up the phone just as Moby walks in the room.

Moby wipes some sweat off his forehead, then glances at the phone. "Everybody ready for tomorrow?"

I dust my hands together. "Yep."

But even if the Arch is just helping with this one plan, I know I'm not ready for how Moby and the rest of the Cadre will react when he shows up.

I tell Moby to meet me early the next morning. The plan is to get to the Dumpsters before the rest of the Cadre and explain what's happening. Hopefully, I'll have time to calm him down by the time everyone else shows up.

Next morning, I meet Moby at our usual spot. Neither of us says a word until we're a block from the school. Then Moby says, "Who do you think stole it?"

I roll my shoulders. "I dunno. I guess somebody who really wants to stick it to Lockhart."

"Why do you think that?"

I consider it for a second. "I guess because that's why I would steal it."

Moby nods. "Yeah."

"Why? Who do you think took it?"

He kicks a rock off the sidewalk and onto the street. "Somebody nobody suspects."

I stop walking and give him a questioning look.

"What? You and the Arch are the main suspects. Why would either of you take it? Lockhart would be all over you."

He starts walking again and I follow.

When we get to the school's parking lot we creep along the wall toward the Dumpsters. It's still early, but we don't want to attract any attention. Once we're safely behind the Dumpsters I set my bag down in a dry spot and take a deep breath. I've tried out a million different ways to tell him about the Arch, but none seems easier than just blurting it out.

"So, listen, Mobe."

He stops buttoning up his sweater and turns toward me.

"Remember on Friday, how . . ." The words freeze in my mouth. Suddenly my blurt-and-pray idea doesn't seem so simple.

"When you were talking about the person who wants to join the Cadre?"

I don't bother to hide my shock. "Uh, yeah."

"Are they coming today?"

"Yeah. That's what I wanted to talk to you about." His shoulders drop a little.

It's now or never. "Wellll, it's the Arch." When the words are out I lean back slightly in case Moby actually explodes.

Several very quiet seconds go by before Moby sucks in a deep breath and says, "Oh, okay."

I relax out of my exploding-best-friend pose. "Wait, you aren't mad?"

"No. Why?"

I shake my head, mystified. "Well, last year you were mad when Shelby joined."

"Because I thought you were going to get a new

best friend. I know that isn't going to happen with the Arch."

"Probably not." I give a small laugh, relieved Moby isn't going to freak out.

Moby laughs too. "*Definitely* not." Then he laughs even louder as he buttons his sweater the rest of the way. The way he says it makes it sound sort of like a threat. "So, what kind of plot do you have cooked up for the Cadre of Evil today?"

"You remember what the Colonel said about Valerie what's-her-name? I think I know how to get Lockhart out of here long enough to get in and hack her computer."

Moby rubs his hands together. "How?"

Before I can answer, a girl's voice comes out of the deepest shadows at the back of the alcove. "Plots, computer hacking, Cadres . . ."

Megumi steps into the shaft of morning light filtering between the two Dumpsters. She has a headlamp on her head and a comic book in her hand. "Whatever you guys are talking about, I want in."

CHAPTER 11

I really need to start carrying a flashlight with me; I don't think my heart can take anyone else popping out of the shadows behind the Dumpsters.

"What are you doing here, Megumi?" My voice wobbles from being startled.

"You told me about this place, remember?"

I remember. It was when I tripped over her feet sticking out of the hedge. "I didn't think you'd actually come here."

She takes off her headlamp and stuffs it into her bag. "Why, because of the smell?"

I'm suddenly embarrassed by exactly how funky

it is back here. I don't want her thinking I'm the kind of person who actually likes hanging out behind Dumpsters. "It's bad right now because it's warm. By November it will be a lot better."

She nods. "Yeah, but it *is* private. And you were right—after a while you don't even smell it anymore."

Moby sucks in a deep breath through his nose. "I don't smell anything."

Megumi covers her mouth and giggles. "See?"

I consider telling her that Moby's nose is immune to bad smells from living with himself for eleven years, but I want her gone before everyone else shows up. She seems like a nice kid; I don't want to get her mixed up in all this. Before I can think of a really good reason to boot her out she says, "Who's the Arch?"

Before I can answer, Moby does. "The Arch isn't really a *who*, so much as—"

"Wait, are you talking about Archer Norris?" she interrupts.

"Yeah, do you know him?" Moby says.

Megumi looks surprised. "You won't believe this,

but he's the only person here other than Chub who has any clue about *Ronin Girl*."

The thought of them looking at the comic together in the halls makes my head get hot.

"Are you and Archer friends?" Megumi asks.

Moby and I scoff at the same time.

"What's so funny?"

For a second it occurs to me that I don't actually know the answer. "It's kind of a long story." I motion toward the exit, but she stays right where she is.

"I like stories. Don't you, Moby?" She sits on her backpack, puts her elbows on her knees, and looks up at me like a little kid ready for a nursery rhyme before bed.

Moby walks over to her side of the alcove and sits down next to her. "I've heard it before, but I'll listen again."

I fold my arms so she'll know I'm serious about what I'm about to say. "I'd love to tell you all about me and the Arch and everything, but we're expecting some people for a private meeting and you probably don't want to know what we're going to discuss."

Megumi wrinkles her forehead. "Why wouldn't I want to know?"

Moby leans toward her and whispers horribly, "Plausible deniability."

She looks at us each once to see if we're serious. When it's clear we are, she stands and dusts off the seat of her pants. "Got it. Private meeting." She heaves her backpack over her shoulder and she's about to slip out the exit when something gets in the way of the light filtering between the Dumpsters. All three of us plaster our backs against the metal boxes. The thing blocking the light moves and a silhouette falls on the back wall of the alcove.

The outline of Lockhart's flattop is unmistakable. She turns her head in both directions, then sniffs the air. The three of us try not to breathe. If she decides to stay and watch the buses unload, nobody else will be able to sneak back here and there won't be a meeting this morning.

She whips her head back and forth one more time, and then calls to the custodian, "Mr. Kraley! I need you to do something about the smell from these

Dumpsters." Her heels clack away quickly, then stop. I can't make out her words but she's going on and on about the smell. What does she expect him to do, wash the garbage?

Megumi leans over to me and whispers, "Looks like I'm staying."

Unfortunately, she's right. We can't risk Lockhart seeing her and finding our hiding spot. I'm about to declare the meeting off and figure out a way to reschedule it when there's a metal clatter and a scraping sound like a shopping cart crashing into a car. It comes from the far end of the parking lot. Lockhart's heels fly toward the sound.

"Go!" I whisper to Megumi, but before she can react Shelby careens into the alcove, pushing Megumi right back in. She's followed a few seconds later by the Arch.

A few seconds after that, the last official member of the Cadre, Sizzler, shows up. He takes up as much space as two average-size seventh graders, so everyone shifts around to make room. When they notice the Arch, Sizzler and Shelby back into a corner as far away from him as they can get. This isn't how I wanted this to go down. I was hoping to have a minute to explain things to everyone before they saw him.

Shelby drops the duffel bag she's carrying, folds her arms, and glares at the Arch, then at me. "What's he doing here?"

I don't have time to tell her everything. "He's here to help."

Something clicks and Shelby's eyebrows shoot up. "Wait! Is this costume for him?" She kicks the bag.

This is going to get out of hand if I don't calm her down. "Listen, guys, I just need you to trust me, okay?"

Shelby flaps her hand toward the Arch like she's trying to dry her feathers. "I trust you, Maciek. It's him I don't trust."

Sizzler nods. "Did you forget about literally everything that happened last year?"

They have every reason not to trust him. I open my mouth to say whatever I need to say to keep the plan on track, but the Arch comes to his own defense.

"Listen, Shirley—"

Shelby slowly turns and pushes her glasses up on her nose. "It's Shell-bee, thank you very much."

"Sorry, Shell-*bee*. I know I'm not your favorite person—"

"True," Sizzler says.

The Arch looks at him, then back at Shelby. "But I didn't steal the Boogerloo, and I have just as much at stake as the rest of you if we don't find the thief. So what do you say? Cut me a little slack. What have you got to lose?" He lowers his head but raises his eyes like a puppy begging for forgiveness.

My plan to get on Lockhart's computer will only work if everyone is on board. I look at Shelby. She gives the Arch the same peer-into-your-soul stare she's used on me in the past. After a few seconds of silent inquisition, she straightens up. "We'll see, we'll see."

The Arch scratches the back of his neck. "Um, okay."

There's rustling in the entry and then the McQueens slip in one by one. When all three of them are in, it becomes impossible to move without rubbing against somebody. If Moby wasn't pinned against the back wall next to Megumi, he probably would've disappeared by now.

The triplets are normally very punctual. "What took you guys so long?"

One of them pulls the substitute hat out of another one's satchel and puts it on. "Sorry, boy-o. There was a dragon guarding the keep. We had to create a distraction so everyone could get in."

Classic McQueens. "What was that noise?"

"We—um, *found* a shopping cart on the way to school." The three of them chuckle. "Tragically, it got loose and crashed into Lockhart's car. I'm sure the scratch will buff out."

I shake my head in fake disappointment. "That's a shame."

"She'll be busy for a bit." He winks, then rubs his hands together. "Did someone say something about a caper?"

They don't mention payment, and I don't offer. They shoot a quick look at the Arch, and then the one with the hat tips it toward him. The McQueens are total professionals. The Arch nods back, an odd look on his face. First I think it's confusion, but then I realize it's something else. He's stuffed into a tiny space, shoulder to shoulder with a group of people who came together last year to take him down. He isn't confused; the Arch is actually nervous. I take a moment to enjoy that, and then I wedge myself between him and Megumi and call the meeting to order.

I point at Shelby's duffel. "Did you get everything we need?"

Shelby fishes in the bag and pulls out a wrinkled page torn from a magazine. She holds up the picture of the artist Wahoolie in front of the Arch and looks back and forth between them.

"I think so. I couldn't tell from the pictures if Wahoolie has a hook for a hand or something else, so he'll have to keep it tucked in the sleeve."

"Wait, what?" the Arch sputters.

I've actually been looking forward to this moment. "You said you wanted to help. This is how we do it."

He taps the picture with the back of his hand. "I don't look anything like that guy."

Shelby snaps the picture back and folds her arms. "Moby doesn't look like a twenty-three-year-old poker player either, but we fooled you, didn't we?"

Moby puffs out his chest and grins.

The Arch sighs and shakes his head. "This'll never work."

Everyone looks at me, concerned. The plan won't work without a Valerie.

"It only has to work for a second. But if you're scared . . ."

"C'mon, Archer," Sizzler says. "You've never been the type to chicken out."

The Arch chews his lip for a second, then kicks the brick wall with his heel. "Fine. Give me the makeup."

Everyone laughs, then remembers that Lockhart might come back at any moment and then goes silent again.

"Sorry to disappoint you, Archer." Shelby unzips her bag and digs inside. "No makeup this time. This role only calls for wardrobe and a goatee."

We need to make sure everything fits and that the Arch looks enough like Wahoolie to fool someone from a hundred yards away. While Shelby dresses him in the costume, I go over the plan with everyone else. Sizzler pulls out the voice-changing gizmo he used when he pretended to be my dad on the phone last year during the Arch's campaign speech.

"Can you make it sound like Wahoolie? He's Australian. That devil-robot voice you used on me will make Mrs. Osborne suspicious."

Sizzler pokes some buttons. "It doesn't do accents. I watched some interviews with him on YouTube, but I can't sound like him."

"Try it once," I say.

He finds the setting he wants, then talks into the thing. The voice that comes out is his, but much deeper. *"Can I talk to the principal?"*

"Whoa!" Moby's eyes go wide.

It sounds pretty cool, but it definitely does not sound Australian. "We'll have to go with Plan B."

The Arch looks impressed. "You have a Plan B? Thorough."

I touch my fingers together. "I always have a Plan B."

He leans as far away from me as he can in the tiny space. "Okaaaay."

I lay out the alternate plan for luring Lockhart to the coffee shop, then give everyone else their assignments.

I've spaced the McQueens out from the parking lot all the way to the courtyard, with Moby closest to the office, so he feels like he's a major part of the operation. If Lockhart leaves the coffee shop too early, it means that my plan to fool her with our fake Wahoolie has failed, and Sizzler will have to race back to signal the first McQueen who is stationed in the parking lot. He will then start a chain of birdcalls when he sees Sizzler's signal, and I'll know I've got less than a minute to get out.

I wish Sizzler, Moby, and the McQueens luck and send them off. A moment later Shelby puts the final touch, a goatee that looks like it was freshly shaved off a poodle's butt, onto the Arch's face.

He presses his lips together to keep beard glue from oozing into his mouth. "This'll never work."

We'll find out at lunch if he's right or wrong. "It only needs to fool her for a second."

Shelby pops a beret on the Arch's head, then stands back to inspect her work.

He doesn't look exactly like the guy, but as the Colonel would say, "It's close enough for government work."

I look the Arch in the eyes. "Do you know what to do?"

He rips the butt-hair beard off his face and hands it back to Shelby, who stashes it in a Ziploc bag for later. "Yeah, don't get caught!"

I push him toward the exit. "We'll meet back here during lunch, after it's done."

He doesn't say a word, just slips out.

Shelby zips up her duffel and moves toward the door. "See you in homeroom."

I wave to her but when I look up she has a scowl on her face. I'm about to ask her what that's about when she turns on her heel and slips out.

"What's her problem?" Megumi asks. I'd forgotten she was still there.

"I have no idea. Well, I hope you enjoyed the meeting. I'm sorry I missed you at lunch yesterday. Maybe we can read *Ronin Girl* after we sort all this out?"

She makes no move to leave.

"Okay, well, I have to go."

She folds her arms. "I told you I want in."

"Well, this plot is full. Maybe next time."

"I don't think you understand, Chub. If you want to read *Ronin Girl*, I'm going with you."

CHAPTER 12

Like most people, when I'm facing a really tough decision, I always ask myself, *What would Captain Kirk do?* Deciding between risking the plan by taking Megumi along and not getting to read *Ronin Girl* is no Kobayashi Maru, but it's one of the hardest choices I've ever had to make. I've learned from years of being friends with Moby that last-minute improvisations are a surefire way to ruin a really good plan. On the other hand, the rarest comic I'll ever see is within reach. My mom always calls things like this "Sophie's choice." I have no clue who this Sophie is, or how my mom knows her, but there's no way she had a tougher decision than the one I'm going to have to make.

The first bell rings, shaking me out of my thoughts.

"So?" Megumi folds her arms. "When are *we* breaking into Lockhart's office?"

I let out a deep sigh. "How about I give you a nice, safe lookout post or something where there's no chance of getting caught?"

She raises her eyebrows. "I'm not worried about getting caught. Are you?"

"No," I say a little too quickly. "But I don't have a choice. I have to go in there. Why would you want to risk it?"

She shrugs. "Maybe I want some excitement in my life, like Ronin Girl. Or maybe I want the thief to get caught too."

Those are two pretty good reasons—not that I have any idea what kind of excitement Ronin Girl gets herself into, since I haven't read it yet.

"Fine. You can stand guard by the door while I watch the video."

She raises her eyebrows at me like I just claimed I could fart the national anthem.

I'm getting annoyed and I have to get to class. The last thing I need is to be tardy and end up in the principal's office for the right reason today. "Did I say something funny?"

"Kinda. Do you think she just has the video sitting on her unlocked desktop with a big play button on it? She'll have some sort of security."

She's right! I spent so much time planning the part about getting Lockhart *out* of the office, I never thought about what I would do if I actually got *in*.

"And I suppose you know how to get around it?"

She smiles. "If this school uses the same formula for passwords that they used over at Trondson, which they probably do, I can get in."

"How do you know the password formula?"

She looks me up and down. "How do you not? It's last name plus their school district employee number. Most of them don't bother to change it. It's worth a try."

I fight back the smile that pulls on my cheeks. Who is this kid? The sound of students rushing to class is dying down. I probably have less than a minute to get to mine, not enough time to convince her to tell me Lockhart's employee number. "All right, you can come," I say. "But if you get caught—"

"I know, I know. You'll disavow any knowledge of my activities."

I pick up my bag. "Also . . . ," but when I turn to finish, Megumi is already gone.

Between morning classes, I see the Arch in the halls a few times. Each time, I throw him a raised eyebrow, and each time he looks away quickly. He probably just doesn't want anyone to see us making nice, but it doesn't make me feel superconfident either way. I pass him again on the way to fourth period, the last class before lunch. I want to make sure he's totally on board, so I shoot him an extra-hard eyebrow that he can't miss. Right before he ducks into a stream of kids, he answers me back with a tiny nod. It'll have to do.

Fourth-period science takes slightly longer than it took humans to evolve from single-cell paramecia. I pack my bag with five minutes left in the period so I can be out the door and ready to go the second the bell rings. When it finally clangs, I race to my locker, stash my bag, and then zoom downstairs to meet Megumi.

She's already in the foyer. She examines the trophy case, especially the bare spot on the middle shelf.

"Lockhart's still in there," she says when I get next to her.

"Is her door open?"

Megumi nods. "I think she likes to eavesdrop on the kids in the hall."

"Perfect," I say. We get in our hiding spot behind the trophy case so Lockhart won't see us if the plan works and she dashes out the door for the coffee shop.

Right on cue Sizzler and the hatted McQueen appear in the hall together. I give them the thumbs-up, and they initiate Plan B.

They walk slowly by the office and stop at the water fountain. In a voice loud enough to hear inside Lockhart's office, Sizzler says, "Jenny Parker's mom just texted her. She's at that coffee shop around the corner, and the guy who made the Boogerloo is there."

I strain to see if I can hear the sound of heels coming from her office.

The McQueen replies. "Patchouli is there now?"

Sizzler covers his mouth to keep from laughing, regains his composure, and says. "It's Wa-hoo-lie. And yeah, he's just chilling over at that coffee shop on Madison right now."

Now there is a commotion coming from the office. The familiar sound of items being thrown in a purse for a quick departure. Sizzler and the McQueen hear it too, and vacate the hall to take up their lookout spots for the next phase of the plan.

We don't have to wait long before Lockhart flies from the office and out the front door in the direction of the coffee shop. Right on her heels, Mrs. Osborne scurries out to go do her lunch monitor duties, only slowing down long enough to lock the knob on the office door. Before she's even around the corner Megumi dashes for the closing door and catches it just before it closes. I check the halls one last time, then slip into the empty office.

As soon as the door shuts behind us, I slap my head when I realize the mistake I just made.

"I forgot about the camera!" I whisper.

Megumi looks annoyed. "I put a gym towel over it before you arrived."

"How'd you get up there?"

Judging by the look on her face, these are stupid questions. "I climbed it."

It looks like bringing her along was the right call.

It'll take Lockhart about four minutes to walk to the coffee shop where our fake Wahoolie is waiting for her. When she walks in, the Arch is supposed to let her see him, then duck into the men's room and sneak out the window while she waits for him to finish. If he plays it right, it'll buy us a few extra minutes. I figure we have at least eight minutes before we need to listen for Moby's birdcall warning us that she's almost here.

The inside of Lockhart's office smells like tea and the despair of three hundred kids. I race around one side of her desk and Megumi goes around the other. Megumi makes an ushering gesture toward the keyboard. I poke a key and the lock screen appears. Her username is filled in, but it's demanding a password.

I look at Megumi. She was right; without her along, I'd be toast right now.

"I got this." She pokes away at the keyboard. "Go listen so we don't miss the signal."

I take up a post by the door and keep my ear out for the cry of a whippoorwill as Megumi presses keys faster than a courtroom reporter.

"Uh, Chub." She looks worried. "It's not working."

"You said you knew how to do it!"

"She isn't using her assigned password. She changed it to something."

Without the password this is a suicide mission. I'm about to call the whole thing off when something catches my eye: the little vomit-nado teacup Lockhart wanted me to see when she brought me in on the first day of school.

"Try 'wahoolie.'"

She shrugs, so I spell it out for her and she punches it in. She stares at the screen for a second, then gives me the same desperate look. "Nope."

I run back to the desk. "Let me try." She looks over my shoulder as I try capitalizing it.

Megumi snaps her fingers. "Wait! It has to be at least ten characters."

My mind goes blank. I check the clock. She's been gone four minutes. It's time to pull the plug. "Let's go. We'll figure out a different way."

Megumi doesn't move. "What's her first name?"

"I don't know! Mizz?"

"Very funny. It's gotta be written somewhere."

I glance at the wall and the first thing I see is what I need. I run over and read the name off her doctorate of education. "It says Gunborg Lockhart. Is that a name?"

"Worth a try." Megumi punches her new idea into the keyboard.

She looks up at me, crosses her fingers, and with the other hand punches the enter key. I expect to see the same disappointed look on her face again, but there's a smile instead. "We're in!"

"No way." I race to the desk

"Way!" Lockhart's desktop is unlocked.

"What was it?"

Megumi makes a sour face. "GunborgWahoolie."

"How did you . . . ?"

"My password used to be MegumiBieber."

"Gross!"

"Don't judge me! Look." She points at the screen, and there in the upper right corner is the icon for the security camera. Megumi clicks it and the program opens, but the view screen is blank.

"What's wrong with the picture?" I ask.

"Towel, remember?" She finds the menu and opens the camera's control panel. She highlights Archived Footage and clicks. Finally, something goes right; there's only one thing saved, last Friday, two forty-five p.m.

She hovers the mouse over the file. "There it is."

"Click it and let's get this over with."

She double clicks the file and the blank screen is replaced with a distorted shot of the hallway and the trophy case. Kids race through the halls in every direction, eager to escape after seven hours in school.

We've been in here too long. "The Boogerloo is still there. Fast forward."

She presses the fast forward button and the hallway empties out in record time. She flips it back to normal speed right after Lockhart strides through the frame and out to the parking lot to supervise the kids getting on the buses.

I check the clock. It's 11:43. She's been gone for eight minutes. She could be back any time now.

I glance at Megumi, and for the first time she looks nervous.

On the footage a shadow falls in front of the trophy case. The thief! My pulse pounds in my ears. The shadow gets smaller as the thief approaches. He or she is almost in the frame when a noise makes me jump.

From the hallway comes a sound like a chicken being hit with a sledgehammer.

Moby. But I'm too close to walk away now.

Megumi grabs my arm. "I think that's the signal. We gotta go, *now*!"

I anchor myself to the desk. "Three more seconds."

And then the thief steps completely in front of the camera. I recognize them immediately. Actually, I should say I recognize *it*. I watch, frozen, as the Gatorade-stained arm of our school's old kangaroo mascot slides open the trophy case, grabs the Boogerloo, and then, before it hops away, waves directly at the camera.

With a numb finger I close the camera program and lock the computer. Another chicken scream echoes in the hallway. It's already too late. I'm planning my next move as I follow Megumi out into the main office. I'm about to tell her to split up and meet by the Dumpsters after school when something stops us both in our tracks.

It's the sound of a key unlocking the office door.

CHAPTER 13

We're trapped like a pair of cockroaches in the middle of the office, and the lights are about to be flipped on. The sound of the key fumbling in the lock makes my pulse redline. My feet are frozen.

Megumi, however, is not. She hops up onto the counter in front of Mrs. Osborne's desk like a cat, then springs again onto a stack of file cabinets. She turns to me, her eyes wide, clearly shocked that I'm just standing there instead of trying to escape. But there's nowhere to go. Her eyes plead with me, but I've already given up on trying to hide. Now I'm trying to figure out what I'm going to say when Lockhart walks through the door.

I glance at Megumi again as the key struggles with the lock.

She mouths "hide," but it's too late. The knob clunks and the door starts to swing open.

Then a buzzing noise hits my ears like a snap of thunder. My first thought is that Lockhart has sounded some sort of secret principal alarm. Then I remember I've heard the sound once before, when the Arch lit the track uniforms on fire last year. The fire alarm. Whoever was opening the door quickly pulls it shut. Over the clanging of the alarm I can barely make out the sound of high heels moving away down the hall.

Megumi bounds down from her perch next to me. "Fire drill?"

I let out a deep breath. "I guess."

"We should wait a minute to make sure the coast is clear," she says.

I nod. My head feels like a bowling ball on a stick. I'm still in shock over how close we came to getting caught. I wait a few seconds, and then creep to the door, inching it open just far enough to see a sliver of the hallway. Halfway down the hall I spot the gray form of Lockhart's pantsuit. Her back is to us as she directs the kids coming from the cafeteria out the door toward the parking lot.

I'm about to tell Megumi this is our chance when she yanks the door wide open and dashes across the hall toward the courtyard. I check one more time to make sure Lockhart's back is still turned, then follow her, making sure to pull the office door closed behind me.

Outside, the fire alarm isn't as deafening. A herd of kids are making their way out of the building in an orderly fashion, so we take up a spot at the back of the group. The adrenaline makes it almost impossible not to grin as we try to look like a pair of ordinary, non-criminal fire drill participants.

As we move through the breezeway that leads from the courtyard to the parking lot, I look at Megumi to make sure she's okay. She seems completely calm, not so much as a bead of sweat on her forehead.

"That was pretty cool, the way you hopped up on the cabinets," I say.

"It's parkour. It's kinda like martial arts, except instead of kicking and punching you use your environment to jump and climb and stuff."

I consider telling her I'm a bit of a martial artist myself, but after what I saw in there, I doubt she'd be impressed. "Where'd you learn that?"

She takes a deep breath. "I've never told anyone this. Can I trust you?"

Does she really need to ask after what we've just been through? I nod.

"When I was four my father sent me away to a secret martial arts school high up on Mount Tanagawa. He left me there until my eighth birthday. They taught me ancient fighting styles and some modern ones as well. My final test was to survive a tiger pit without any weapons. Thankfully, I'd taken parkour as one of my electives. If I hadn't, I'd be tiger poop right now."

"Really?!"

She stops walking and puts a hand on my shoulder. "No. I taught myself by watching videos on

YouTube." She gives me a cheesy grin that shows all of her teeth, then starts walking again. "I told you, my dad leaves me alone a lot. I try to channel my energy so I don't go getting myself in trouble when I'm not supervised."

With every kid at Alanmoore in the parking lot, it isn't easy to find my homeroom group. I steer a wide path around Lockhart, who's still busy directing traffic, and eventually find Mrs. Badalucco and the rest of our homeroom class over by the buses. While she counts heads, I look for the rest of the Cadre. I find Shelby first; her giraffe-like neck makes her easy to spot in a crowd.

She sees me too and pushes toward me. "Chub, what happened in there? Did the fire drill ruin everything?"

"Actually, Lockhart came back early, and it saved us from getting caught in the office."

Shelby straightens up and gives me her patented bird-girl stare. "Who's 'we'?" I don't have to answer, because right then she spots Megumi behind me. "First you bring in the Arch, and now her? I thought you didn't like to improvise."

"I didn't have a choice. I'm actually lucky she was there."

"Well. Isn't. She. Something?" Shelby says.

Thankfully, Moby appears and breaks up the awkwardness. "What the heck?! Didn't you hear my birdcall?"

I wrinkle my forehead at him. "Oh, I heard *something*."

He shrugs. "Yeah, I tried to figure out a whippoorwill last night, but my lips are too chapped to whistle, so . . ."

I shake my head.

"Also," he says, "I don't know how to whistle. So that pretty much leaves chickens or crows. A crow inside a middle school, that'd be weird right?"

I wave my hand, cutting him off. "It doesn't matter. The fire drill saved us so there was no harm done." *Other than some collateral damage to my underwear.* "The Arch must not have made a very convincing Wahoolie. She was barely gone eight minutes."

Shelby looks miffed. "Well, the costume wasn't the issue."

I agree. I saw the dress rehearsal; it was pretty good.

I'm about to ask if anyone else knows what happened when a voice comes from the other side of the ivy-covered fence. "Chub?"

I turn and try to look through the leaves. "Archer?"

"Yeah. It's me and Sizzler. Is she around?"

I don't need to ask who "she" is. I quickly scan the parking lot and spot Lockhart walking around the corner with a firefighter who responded to the alarm. Mrs. Badalucco is distracted talking to the new band teacher. "No. What are you doing?"

The ivy thrashes and a second later both of them drop over the fence.

"What the heck happened?" I ask.

The Arch is short of breath. "What happened is she's the fastest old lady alive!"

"Did she catch you?"

"No, but it was really close. I was in the coffee shop waiting for her. I saw her a block away, and she saw me. She got this weird smile on her face, and before I could stand up and push in my chair, she was right there, in the coffee shop."

Shelby folds her arms and gives him a dubious look.

"I'm not kidding. She's like the T-1000 and the Predator had a baby! She was pounding on the bathroom door when I went out the window."

Sizzler takes over from there. "I wasn't even to my lookout spot yet and Archer flies by me, booking it back here to warn you."

I look around to make sure we aren't overheard. "What'd you guys do?"

The Arch says, "We sprinted up the alley behind Hong's market and cut through the gym. Sizzler was ahead of me, so he went to signal the McQueens, you know, like we'd talked about. I didn't know what else to do, so I just pulled the fire alarm." He stops to catch his breath again.

Shelby fires up the inquisition stare and aims it at the Arch. "Wait, you ran past him, but he made it to the school first?"

The Arch gives her a confused look. "Yeah, why?"

Shelby shakes her head in mock disapproval. "It

appears someone's spot on the track team may be in jeopardy this year."

Shelby pats Sizzler's arm and he smiles, showing off more food selections in his braces than Alanmoore's cafeteria.

I thought Moby or the McQueens had pulled the alarm. "The alarm saved us. We were caught in the office, and she was unlocking the door when you pulled it."

The Arch gives me the same odd look Shelby had a moment before. "We?"

Megumi materializes out of the crowd and gives a shy wave. "Hi."

The Arch straightens up and the look of panic suddenly drains from his face. "Oh, hey, Megumi." His voice is all phony, all *the Arch*.

Megumi smiles back at him. Shelby and I both roll our eyes.

Then Moby pipes up. "Wait, you never told us if you saw the video."

Now Megumi looks at me and raises an eyebrow.

In all the excitement I forgot what we were after in the first place. "We saw it."

Everyone leans in, eyes wide.

"Well, do you know who the thief is?" Shelby practically yells.

I look around to make sure no one is listening, then lean in. "Kind of."

Shelby throws her hands up. "What does that mean?"

"It means everyone knows the thief. It was the Alanmoore kangaroo mascot with the stain on the arm."

The Arch takes a step toward Moby and puffs out his chest. "Wait, the one *he* used when he tried to poison the track team by putting soap in the Gatorade last year?!"

I nod.

"So what are we waiting for? Let's turn him in and get this over with."

Moby looks from me to the Arch and back. "Wait, what?"

I put up my hand. "Relax, Archer. It wasn't Moby."

The Arch takes half a step back, and Moby lets out a small sigh of relief.

Then Megumi says, "It could've been literally anyone in the suit. There's no way to prove it wasn't him, or even you for that matter. You don't have any idea who it was."

But I remember something Margot Mercedes said to me at the Clairmont, and without meaning to, I touch my fingertips together. "I might not know who it was, but I know someone who does."

CHAPTER 14

The rest of the afternoon I avoid the hallway in front of the office as if it were filled with dentists wearing clown masks. Lockhart obviously realized she'd been set up by a fake Wahoolie, and if she was fired up enough to beat the Arch in a footrace back to school while wearing high heels, I don't want to bump into her.

After the final bell I rendezvous with Moby in the parking lot to walk home. I don't want to call the Getter from my house, so I'm hoping we can go to his place instead.

Moby looks sheepish. "So what do we do now?" he asks.

I look around to make sure there aren't any authority figures lurking nearby, then urge him around the corner with a jerk of my head. When we're behind the ivy-covered fence the Arch climbed over earlier, I say, "When I met with Margot Mercedes at the Clairmont last week she told me something that I totally forgot about until this afternoon."

Moby's jaw slackens. "Whoa!"

"I haven't even told you what she said yet."

He closes his mouth and shakes his head like he's clearing out cobwebs. "Sorry. What did she tell you?"

"She told me she didn't have the Boogerloo, but that she had just sold the old kangaroo mascot costume with a Gatorade stain up one arm."

I give him time to put it together on his own. After several seconds without one, something like realization hits him and his jaw flops open again.

He stops walking, looks at the ground, and puts on his most focused look. After a minute he tries and fails to snap his fingers. "Wait! Are you saying Mr. Kraley, the janitor, who usually wears that costume, stole the Boogerloo?"

I slap my forehead. "What? No! I'm saying Margot knows who the thief is because she sold them the suit last week. We have to convince her to tell us who she sold the suit to, and there's the thief."

We start walking again. It's quiet for a second, then Moby says, "Or Margot stole it and she's just trying to throw you off."

I think back to the two-second glimpse I got of the surveillance video. It could've been *almost* anyone, but I doubt it was the shortest kid in school. Still, if your looks are a dead giveaway, you'd probably wear some sort of disguise during a daring daylight caper.

"I don't consider her a suspect just yet; let's call her a person of interest."

I think we're alone on the stretch of sidewalk, so the voice behind me makes me flinch.

"I hope you aren't talking about me."

Megumi is a little too good at appearing out of nowhere and making me *download a folder* in my shorts.

"Geez, Megumi. You gotta stop sneaking up on me like that."

She gives me a raised eyebrow. "I'd think a smooth criminal like you would be a little bit better at looking over his shoulder," she replies. "Hi, Moby."

I half expect Moby to have disappeared into Hong's market when I turn around, but to my surprise he's still there. I have to give him a second look; I'm almost positive the top button of his shirt wasn't buttoned a second ago.

"Hey," he says. I think it might be the first time I've ever heard him directly address a female besides his mom, or Shelby.

For the second time today Megumi uses her sleeve to wipe sweat off my head. "Seriously, dude. The flinching, the sweating. For a guy who claims to be innocent, it's not a good sign."

I look at Moby for backup, but he just shakes his head. "Innocent people don't usually sweat."

Of course, the fact that everyone is staring at my head only makes it sweat even more. "Moby, you've known me for years. I'm always sweaty!"

Megumi laughs. "Chub, we know you're innocent. We're just messing with you. Right, Moby?"

Confusion washes over him. "Oh, right. I was totally just messing with you."

"You guys are too funny," Megumi says. She taps Moby's arm and he freezes like one of those goats that faint whenever you open an umbrella. "So who's this 'person of interest'?"

My instinct tells me not to say too much, but she knows what's on the video already. "I know someone who knows who bought the kangaroo suit."

Megumi's eyes go wide. "The one the thief was wearing?"

I nod.

"Wait, how do you know that this *someone* knows who bought it?"

"Because she told me."

Megumi looks stunned by the revelation. "Well if you know who it was, why haven't you turned them in?"

"She didn't tell me who bought it, only that she sold it to someone. That's what we're going to Moby's house to find out right now."

Moby raises his hand like he has a question.

"What, Mobe?"

"We can't go to my house today. I have a colonic at four."

By the way Megumi winces, a colonic probably isn't something I want to tag along to. Then again, his parents usually pay whenever we go do stuff. . . .

Megumi grimaces. "What kind? Water?"

Moby shakes his head. "Coffee."

She sucks air through her teeth. "Oooh, brutal."

"It is what it is," Moby says.

I hate to interrupt their sidebar, but I need to get the Getter fast, and my best option for calling her is going out for coffee right when I need him most. Then something dawns on me. "I guess I could go to the Clairmont to call her."

Moby looks too distracted by his coffee outing to reply.

Megumi seems confused. "That dumpy old theater? Why would you go there?"

I don't really want any more people at school knowing about our private spot, so I stall.

Then Moby jumps in. "His cousin is the manager. It's kind of our hangout. We get to watch movies before they're released. It's pretty awesome."

Megumi looks impressed. She pushes up her lower lip and bobs her head back and forth like she's weighing some options. "That's a pretty long walk. We could go all the way over there, or we could go two short blocks to my house."

I do like the idea of less exercise. Plus, she might have even more awesome comics there. "What's the parent situation?"

"Like I've told you, Dad's never home. My stepmom, Kendra, is probably out doing yoga with her shih tzu or something. I'm not supposed to have people over, but I don't really care."

With Moby's house burnt as an option, the decision is pretty simple. After recommending he go with decaf so he can sleep tonight, I say good-bye to Moby, and Megumi and I head off toward her house.

Megumi doesn't talk, so I say, "How'd you get into comics?"

She pauses for a second, then replies, "My dad's

majorly into them, so they're always around at the house."

The thought of a parent being not only a fan of minimal supervision but of comic books too makes my head swim. The feeling is like what I imagine it's like to unwrap a Christmas present and see that it's exactly what you asked for, not some slightly weird dollar-store knock-off.

"That's pretty cool that your dad's into comics."

She shrugs. "I guess. What are your parents into?"

Part of me wants to make something up, but what's the point? "They like coupons and helping me build my character."

She tries to look like that's not the worst thing she's ever heard, but pity shows on her face. "So, do those things take up most of their free time?"

I laugh, and then she does too.

"Not all of it. My mom makes czarnina and kiszka for the older people in the Polish club, too."

"What are those?"

Now's my chance to confess some of my family's deepest secrets. Hopefully, she still lets me into her house after this. "Kiszka is blood sausage, and czarnina is duck blood soup. I know it sounds weird, but they're actually both really good."

I watch her face, waiting for the nausea to set in. It doesn't. Instead she just nods. "I'd try it," she says.

I can't hide my shock. "You would?"

"Yeah. Why not?"

"I guess I just figured you'd think it was disgusting, like everyone else does."

She gives me a look that says I've just said something dumb. "We lived in Japan until I was eight. Trust me, we ate stuff that people here would think is a lot weirder than that. I do have one question. Where does your mom get all that blood?"

One thing my dad and I see eye to eye on is that neither of us wants to go shopping with my mom. I'd rather discuss where babies come from with my grandparents than go to the store with her. "I don't know where she gets it."

"So for all you know your parents are vampires."

I try to imagine my mom chasing down and feeding on anything more agile than a bowl of soup. "I guess."

"And having vampire parents is way cooler than having one who's into comics."

It's the first time I've told anyone other than Moby one of my Polish secrets, and suddenly I don't feel quite as different as I did just a few minutes ago.

A block later we are walking along the high, ivy-covered stone wall that separates the area's fanciest neighborhood, Maplehurst, from the rest of the city.

Megumi pats my shoulder. "We're almost there."

I look around. There's nothing but stores and the wall. Then I realize where she's taking me. "You live in Maplehurst?"

She looks embarrassed. "Yeah."

I've never been behind the wall, but I've dreamed about what the houses in there look like. I instantly conjure a picture of a stone castle with a million fire-places and decide that's where Megumi lives. I'm so wrapped up in thought I don't even realize she's stopped walking. I turn and go back where she's stand-ing next to the wall.

"It's through here." She puts her hands into the ivy, spreads it a little, and then steps through and disappears. I put my hands in the same spot and step through it too. I pass through an old archway in the wall that has probably been hidden for so long that nobody except Megumi knows it's still there. We come out on the other side in a backyard that looks like a golf course.

"Is this your house?"

She shakes her head. "No, but it's the only shortcut through the wall. C'mon." She leads me along a fence to a gate, and we slip through it. Once we are out of the backyard I get my first good look at Maplehurst. It's even more spectacular than I imagined.

The houses are old and majestic, with lots of columns and big windows. I'm pretty sure my mouth hangs open as I follow her down the street, gawking at the houses. We turn down a cul-de-sac. There's room for about a dozen versions of my house on the street, but there are only three of them here. The ones on the left and right don't catch my eye, but the one in the center does. It looks like a slightly smaller version of Wayne Manor, where Batman lives when he isn't Batmanning, complete with even more ivy covering one entire side. The best part is we're heading straight for it.

Megumi punches a code into the keypad on the front door and lets us in. We walk into a room that really seems like there should be a butler leading you through it.

"Welcome to mi casa." She waves her hand in a sarcastic imitation of a model on a game show showing off a prize.

I've never been in a house this big before. It even makes Alanmoore feel cramped. For a second I wonder if she doesn't see her dad very much because he can't find her in such a huge house.

"Wow, your house is . . ." I can't come up with big enough word.

"Ridiculous? I know. My dad thinks that buying a huge, stupid museum like this place makes up for a lack of actual parenting. Pretty lame."

It sounds like a decent trade-off to me, but I keep that to myself.

We pass a huge glass table in the middle of the entryway and Megumi flips through the pile of mail sitting on it. She picks out a large envelope and rips it open. "This is interesting."

"What?"

She reads the shiny brochure she pulled from the envelope. "Emerald Con. It's next week. Do you want to go?"

Emerald Con is the annual comic book convention in Seattle. I would probably lop off and sell up to four of my toes to be able to go. "Seriously?"

She tosses the papers back onto the table. "I'll get us tickets if you want."

I try to answer, but the sound that comes out isn't an actual word.

"I'll take that as a yes. Do you want something to eat?" She doesn't wait for me to answer. She spins and darts off. Her voice echoes back to me from down a long hall. "Go in the room with the double glass doors. I'll be there in a sec."

"Okay," I call back. "Can I use your phone while I'm waiting?"

There's silence, so I'm about to ask again when she replies, "Food first."

I guess it won't hurt to have a quick snack before I make the call to Margot. I cross the foyer and push open the glass doors. The room looks like a social club where old-time gangsters would play cards and smoke cigars. An immense wooden desk takes up the end of the room right in front of a wall of floor-to-ceiling windows. The rest of the walls are lined with shelves crammed with enough books to keep Kyle the library wonder boy busy until he's old enough to grow a beard. Instead of the fuzzy, cottage cheese–looking ceilings in my house, the ceiling in here is made of a dark wood that shines like a basketball court. As if it couldn't get any better, there's a TV bigger than my parents' mattress hanging off the wall opposite the desk. I head toward it and gently sit on the couch in front of it. I've never had my butt hugged, but the feeling of sitting on that couch is the closest thing I can imagine to it.

My eyes wander to the end table next to the couch. There's a picture of a guy in a cheesy cheek-to-cheek pose with a young woman. I can't say I recognize him, but something about his face is familiar.

Megumi kicks open the doors and comes into the room, her arms loaded with snacks. She dumps them on the couch and then dusts off her hands. "That'd be cool if you could go to Emerald Con with me."

She's almost acting like I'm the one doing her the favor. "What are friends for?"

She opens a box of Pocky, pulls out all of them in a bunch, and bites off the end. "I wouldn't waste a ticket on a poser, but it seems like you know your stuff."

I open a bag of chips and grab a few. I don't want to appear too eager, but going to Emerald Con is slightly more important to me than things like going to college, or maybe air. "I've been meaning to go for a long time, but I've never been able to make it. I think tickets are, like, seventy-five dollars."

"Well, if you know *Ronin Girl*, you deserve to go. Consider it an early—or late—birthday present."

I look around the room again and my eye settles on the photo once more. Something about the guy throws up a flag in my head.

Megumi crunches on some chips behind me. "It should be a good Con this year. Lots of big names."

Then something clicks and I suddenly realize why I recognize the guy in the picture. "That's Tatsuo Kobayashi. He wrote *Ronin Girl*."

I turn to Megumi and she nods.

"You weren't kidding about your dad being into comics. I mean, the picture isn't autographed or anything, but that's still pretty cool. I thought *I* was a fanboy."

When I turn around Megumi has a serious look on her face. Great, it took me less than a minute to mess up my invite to Emerald Con.

"Megumi, did I say something wrong?"

She takes a deep breath. "My dad's not a fan, Chub."

"Then why does he have Kobayashi's picture in his office? And who's the lady?"

She rolls her eyes. "The lady is my stepmother."

I gasp. "She met Kobayashi? When?"

"Oh, about three months before she married him."

CHAPTER 15

You know that expression "My head is swimming"? When I put together what she's telling me, my head doesn't swim, it flails around like the people in the adult swimming lessons I saw at the YMCA once. It's not so much swimming as drowning without dignity.

"Your dad is Tatsuo Kobayashi!"

"Wow, can't fool you."

"But . . . ," I sputter, "why didn't you tell me?"

She rolls her eyes. "If I had a mirror right now you'd understand."

I'm suddenly aware of the contortions on my face.

I check my lower lip. There isn't a lot of drool, but I wipe what's there away with my sleeve anyway. The picture is under a lamp so I lean in close to examine it. I never noticed the resemblance between him and Megumi before. But then again, why would I?

"So, that means this is his office?"

She sighs a perturbed sigh. "With those detective skills, I can't believe you haven't found the Boogerloo yet."

Normally a comment like that would make my scalp bead up with sweat, but nothing can ruin the feeling I have right now. I am in the personal office of one of the great artists of our time. I spring from the couch and run/walk to the desk. "Is this where . . . ?"

She nods. "When he's here."

I scan the desk, hoping for a glimpse of a work in progress. I'd even settle for a small doodle on the corner of a scratch pad. Unfortunately, the desk is more organized than the Colonel's sock drawer.

"Where is he?"

"I told you, Chub. He's never here."

The way her face darkens makes me very aware of

the silly grin I have plastered all over mine. I do my best to get rid of it, but the most I can manage is to smash it down into a small smirk.

Megumi comes over to the other side of the desk. "So, now you know my secret."

By the look on her face, she thinks her big secret is a lot more embarrassing than it is. If we were to have an embarrassing-secret contest, I would win in a landslide. I wouldn't even have to dig that deep. I could beat this with a small one like, "Sometimes when I push a fart a little too aggressively, I have to hide my underwear in the middle of the laundry basket and hope my mom doesn't see it before she tosses it in the machine."

I compose myself. "Why don't you want people to know who your dad is?"

"Everybody thinks they know him just because they've read some of his comics. He's my dad and *I* don't even really know him." She looks away. "Sometimes when people at school find out who he is they get all . . . weird." She gives me a look. "Some of them even literally drool."

I flush, embarrassed. There must be some good

things about having a famous dad. I bet she's never been woken up at five o'clock in the morning by the sound of prehistoric radiator pipes popping as they warm up. (It sounds like a monkey destroying the plumbing section of Home Depot, in case you've never heard it.)

Then something occurs to me. "Wait, why do you go to a dump like Alanmoore? How come you don't go to a private school?"

"I went to one of those schools when we lived in Tokyo. It was even worse than public school. At places like that everyone's parents are *somebody*, and everyone finds out who's who sooner or later. Those schools might be in nicer buildings, but they are just as bad when it comes to ranking everyone by status."

I'd never even considered that. I guess I always assumed that the more money you have, the easier your life is. Still, living in a house like this probably wouldn't completely suck. It would have to be better than your parents never being more than fifteen feet away.

Then something hits me. "Megumi, if you don't want anyone to know who he is, why'd you bring me over here and let me into his office?"

She shrugs. "I never said I don't want *anyone* to know. I said I don't want *everyone* to know."

That makes my face hot again. "Why me?"

"I don't know. I guess I like the way you fight back when the system is wrong. Reminds me of *Ronin Girl*, you know?"

I nod, but the truth is I *don't* know. I still haven't gotten to read it, and I'm starting to wonder if I ever will. I almost ask her if now would be a good time, but considering what she just told me, I don't want to upset her by bringing up her dad again. The best thing for now is to use her phone to call the Getter and then get out of here before I say something dumb and mess up my invite to Emerald Con.

I'm scanning the office for a phone when she says, "Who do you think was in the kangaroo costume?"

My first thought is that it was the Arch, but after he singlehandedly saved us from getting caught in the office by pulling the fire alarm, it doesn't feel right to accuse him.

"I have a couple of theories," I lie, hoping she doesn't ask me what they are.

She nods. "I guess you have to ask yourself why someone would do it. I mean, you and the Arch are the ones with the reputations for that sort of thing—everyone knows that—so doesn't that sort of rule you out? Why would you commit a crime knowing you'd be the first ones to get hauled in?"

I say what I've been thinking ever since I first saw that the Boogerloo had disappeared. "Unless one of us wanted to frame the other."

She bites her lip. "I don't buy it; too risky. You're both smarter than that."

"Okay, so what's your theory?"

"Maybe this has nothing to do with Lockhart."

I've been so worried about proving my innocence that it never occurred to me. "I'm listening."

"I'm just saying, maybe it's someone you've never thought of, for a reason you've never thought of."

I'm not sure where she's going with this, but I don't like it. "What are you saying, exactly?"

She spins and walks back toward the couch. "Think about it, Chub. You hang out with a bunch of kids who have all kinds of experience pulling capers at school.

Is it so weird to think it might be one of the people you meet with behind the Dumpsters?"

That makes my head break out in a full sweat. Nobody in the Cadre would do something like that without telling me, would they?

Megumi throws her legs over the arm of the couch and flops back, staring at the ceiling. "Can you think of a reason why one of them would do it?"

It feels like I'm betraying my friends to even think it, but I run through a checklist in my head. Not the McQueens; Lockhart succeeded in putting the fear of God into them.

Sizzler might still want to get back at the Arch for stealing his golden-boy status on the track team last year, but he's bigger than most adults I know. If it had been him in the suit, it would've been obvious.

That leaves only Shelby and Moby. In my wildest dreams, I can't imagine one of them doing something that bold.

"I don't think so, Megumi."

"All I'm saying is you can't know for sure until you know for sure."

Moby *was* mad at me last year when Shelby joined the Cadre, but we've been cool ever since. And there's no way Megumi could know about that anyway. That only leaves . . .

"Shelby?"

She shrugs. "I just wouldn't rule out anyone whose alibi isn't ironclad."

"Great! That means I'm the only one I can be sure about."

Megumi stands up and dusts off her hands. "I'm sure you'll figure it out." She gathers up the mostly untouched snack packages from the couch.

"Can I use the phone while I'm here?"

She looks around like it might be lying on the floor. "Let me go find it." She goes out and leaves me to soak in the mystique of Kobayashi's den.

A section of the bookcase catches my eye. The books on the shelf don't look like the others. I float toward them like I'm on a remote-controlled hoverboard. I've seen spines like that before; they're the kind of albums serious collectors use to catalog things like magazines and rare comic books. I tilt one of the volumes slightly out of its place on the shelf to inspect it. My heart flutters like a moth in my chest when I see the neat rows of vinyl slipcovers, each filled with colorful pulp pages.

I wait for the rush of my pulse in my ears to calm, then strain to hear any clue as to where Megumi is in the house. After a few seconds of silence, I'm rewarded by the sound of a drawer opening in a distant room. I quickly slide the album off the shelf, carefully open the cover, and get my first glimpse at the personal collection of Tatsuo Kobayashi.

I have no clue what I am looking at. I know only two things: it is awesome, and I wish I knew how to read Japanese. Unfortunately, I don't, so it makes no sense to me. The album is full of other issues of the same comic, which as far as I can tell is about an angry octopus-god who fights a legion of giant cyborgs. As quickly as possible I replace the volume and move over a few shelves to see what other treasures he has hidden in here.

I randomly pick another album and carefully slide it out of the shelf.

"I see you found his collection," Megumi says.

She's standing right next to me and her voice makes me jump. The album leaps out of my hands like a frog. I grab for it, but Megumi snags it out of midair before I get the chance.

"Are you trying to give me a heart attack, Megumi?"

"No." She holds up a phone with her other hand. "I was trying to give you this."

"Thanks." I go to take the phone from her, but she pulls it back.

"Can I ask you something, Chub?"

I'd rather wait until after I talk to the Getter, but she looks pretty serious. She's working up the nerve to say what she has to say when the sound of the front door opening echoes from the front hall. Megumi snatches the phone and tosses it on the couch.

"What are you doing?"

Her forehead wrinkles with worry. "That's my stepmom. I'm not allowed to have anyone over when they aren't home."

At least there's one thing our parents have in common.

Her eyes plead with me. I shoulder my bag and then follow her to the open window.

A voice like a goose with a sinus infection pierces the air from the front hall. "Gumi, you home, baby?"

Megumi takes my bag and tosses it into the bushes outside the window. "You have to go now!"

I do my best to mount the windowsill without embarrassing myself, but I can't get my leg over without Megumi pushing on my butt. When I'm halfway out I turn to her. "When will I see you again?"

"Probably tomorrow at school." Before I can say anything else she shoves me the rest of the way out the window.

I try to stick the landing like Iron Man, but when I hit the ground it's more like a turd falling out of the back end of a horse.

When she closes the window above me, I crawl out of the bushes I've fallen into and dust myself off. I still need to call the Getter, and with Moby out getting coffee, Shelby's house is my next best bet. I don't want to believe it, but maybe she has something she wants to tell me before I make the call.

CHAPTER 16

I shove myself through the hole in the wall and pop out onto the sidewalk. Even though Maplehurst is only a few feet away, the air smells completely different. In there it smelled like flower gardens and just-watered grass. Out here it smells like asphalt and exhaust.

It takes me a second to get my bearings, then I start off toward Shelby's house. I only have a few blocks to figure out how to approach her about this. Is it even possible that Shelby took the Boogerloo? She *has* been on edge lately, but that doesn't prove anything.

By the time I get to her house I've decided how

I'm going to rule her out as a suspect without making her mad. My Uncle Stosh always said, "Honesty is the best policy." But since in this case honesty might earn me a severe case of bird-girl wrath, it's safer to go with the second-best policy: snooping.

Shelby's Grammie opens the door before I'm even done knocking. Her wrinkled cheeks pull back like theater curtains when she sees me. "Hello, Chad!"

"Um, it's Chub, actually."

She looks confused for a second, then shakes her head and invites me in. "Shelby is in her room. I'm sure she'd love a caller."

"I don't have a cell phone. Can I just go talk to her?"

Her confused look returns. "Okay." She gestures down the hall.

I don't have to ask which room is Shelby's. The first door I come to has a theater poster tacked to it. It's written in French or something. The only word I recognize is "Miserable." This is definitely her room. I knock.

"Come in, Grammie," Shelby calls from inside.

I crack the door, praying like heck that she isn't changing clothes or something. "It's not Grammie. It's Chub."

I'm about to open the door all the way when the handle is yanked out of my hand, pulling me off balance. I stagger into Shelby's room.

"What are you doing here, Maciek?"

I try to sound casual. "I just came by to say hi."

She looks surprised. "Oh . . . hi."

I take a quick look around the room. I'm not sure what I expected, but this isn't it. I guess I figured there'd be doilies and vases and stuff to go along with the granny way she dresses, but instead the walls are plastered with posters and magazine pages.

"Where's Moby?"

"He's out with his mom. Just me."

"Well, this is a nice surprise."

One of the pictures catches my eye and I step past her toward it. It looks like Hugh Jackman, but he's wearing a leopard-print shirt and holding a pair of maracas. "Is that Wolverine? I didn't know you liked comic book movies."

She lets out an annoyed breath. "I don't, but I am a fan of a multiple-Tony-Award-winning actor who happens to play in one occasionally."

The rest of the pictures on the walls are similar, but I don't recognize any of the people in them. I pull out a small stool in front of a three-sided mirror and sit. "This is a nice room."

Shelby wrinkles her nose. "No it isn't."

She's right, but something tells me this isn't the thing to suddenly agree with her about.

"Did you come over to check on my decorating skills, or was there another reason?"

"I don't know. You've been kinda grumpy lately and I thought I'd check on you."

Her mattress sits directly on the floor, and as my Uncle Stosh would've said, "The room is so small you'd have to go outside to change your mind." If Shelby was hiding the Boogerloo, the only place to stash it in here would be the closet. Unfortunately, the closet doors are closed.

"Well, there's been a lot going on. But we don't need to ruin this visit talking about that."

Thank God.

She runs her hand over her dress to smooth out the wrinkles. "Grammie and I were about to watch *Masterpiece Theater*. They're airing a production of *Othello* from the National Theatre in London."

She may as well be speaking Swahili. Not one word of that made sense to me. "Oh, cool."

"It's a play. You could watch it with us if you want."

I'd probably agree to watch something as horrible as ballet if it would get her out of the room for a minute. "Sounds good."

Shelby puts her hands together like she's about to pray and claps them excitedly. "You'll love it! I swear."

"I knew you were in theater club and everything, but I didn't know how much you were into it."

She looks down. "I'm interested in lots of things, in case you never noticed."

I look around the room again for a clue about what else she might be into. Unless she's into peeling wallpaper, or piles of clothes, I have no clue what she's talking about.

After a moment of awkward silence, she looks at

the picture of Hugh Jackman. "Life isn't always about comics, you know."

She's right. Lately mine has been about everything but. The whole Boogerloo situation has me nostalgic for the days when I knew exactly who my nemesis was and I could spend my time plotting his downfall. This year was supposed to be even better. This year I was supposed to stay out of trouble completely.

The sooner I find that stupid glass blob, the sooner I can start my life as just another Alanmoore student. I need her out of the room so I can check the closet.

I force an eager smile onto my face. "Hey, does your Grammie have any of those cookies she had last time I was here?"

Shelby perks back up. "I think so. Perfect theater food. Good idea!" She turns to go.

The cookies were slightly more difficult to swallow than a stick of sidewalk chalk. I poke my head out her door and call, "Can you bring something to drink, too?"

Her reply is a sing-song call. It comes from the kitchen, so I have a minute to myself.

I move to the closet door and inch it open. The door makes a sound like the one Moby made that time he forgot to wear underwear and zipped up his pants too quickly. I freeze, listening for footsteps in the hall. When there aren't any, I inch the closet door open more, lifting on the knob to keep the hinge from giving me away.

Down the hall, a pantry door slams. She'll be back any minute. If she catches me in her closet I will be toast.

I press my eye to the opening and peer inside. It takes a second to adjust to the dark, but when it does, I see what I should've expected to see: rows of sweaters neatly hung on hangers and a small rack of old lady shoes on the ground. I'm about to call it clear when something in the back corner catches my eye.

Something purple.

My heart races. I quickly listen toward the hall for any sound, then reach in closer for the purple thing, making sure I don't move the noisy door.

Suddenly I hear footsteps approaching. I stretch toward the back corner of the closet. With one last push, I grab it. I expect to wrap my hand around the silly glass blob. Instead I feel . . . feathers?

I yank my hand out of the closet just as Shelby glides into the room with a plate of cookies.

She gives me a confused look. "What are you doing?"

I look around, desperately searching for an excuse, and my eyes land on a poster from another play. "Is Wolverine in that one too?" I ask, pointing at the poster.

Shelby takes a step toward it and sets the cookie plate on the bed. I look at my hand and my heart skips. It's covered in small purple feathers.

"No, that one's with Matthew Broderick." She admires the poster.

I cram my hand in the pocket of my sweatshirt, trying to wipe off the feathers. "Hmm," I say, pretending to contemplate Matthew Broderick, my pulse racing.

Shelby goes on. "He became famous playing teenage nogoodniks, but *he* matured and now he's a Broadway star." Her arms fold like a pair of wings and she swivels her neck around like I'm supposed to be impressed.

"So, he used to be in movies, but now he's just in plays? That sounds like a demotion to me."

She rolls her eyes

"Sorry, I don't know anything about plays and culture stuff."

"It's okay; it's an acquired taste." Her head cocks to one side and she reaches down and picks something off the floor. She straightens up and holds her hand in front of me. Between her fingers is a small purple feather.

My head starts to sweat as she turns on the inquisition stare. I blurt out the first thing that comes to mind. "Ooh, pretty."

Shelby whirls around toward the closet. The door is still cracked open. *Was it totally shut before I looked inside?*

When she turns back to me, the stare is turned up to eleven. "Were you in my closet?"

She's locked onto me like a tractor beam. I can't look away, but I can't lie to her either. She's been lied to enough to know what one looks like. Then her stare suddenly fades, replaced by a look I know all too well: disappointment. She flops down on the edge of the bed and wraps her arms around her knees. She twirls the feather between her fingers. "I'm such a fool."

It looks like there could be tears at any moment, and I'm not ready for that with all the other stuff on my mind. I slide my foot toward the door.

"Here I thought you might want my help, but you came over to see if I stole the Boogerloo?"

She'd see right through me if I tried to deny it. It's probably best if I just call the Getter and then give her some time alone.

I wipe some sweat off my head with my sleeve. "Shelby, I didn't think you took it, but I had to be sure."

"So you thought the best way to be sure was to come over here under false pretenses and then snoop through my room?"

Embarrassment hits me. The day Shelby joined me and Moby in our quest to take down the Arch was the day we officially became a Cadre. Have I really become desperate enough to spy on someone I trust? "I'm sorry, Shelby. I didn't know what else I was supposed to do."

She stands up and looks down at me. "Did you ever think to just ask me?"

I look around the room one last time. There is nowhere else to stash the thing. "Well?"

She narrows her eyes. "Well, what?"

"Did you take the Boogerloo?"

The silence in the room is so deep I could probably hear a butterfly fart a block away. I wish I could take back the question, but the hurt look on her face makes my stomach flop. I'm afraid to say anything else and make it worse.

After a small eternity, Shelby goes to the door and slowly pulls it open. "I was wrong, Maciek. I'm not the fool. You are."

As usual, Shelby's right.

CHAPTER 17

I could walk the ten blocks to the Clairmont to call the Getter, but that would flagrantly break my New Year's resolution to get *less* exercise. Besides, the clock is ticking and Moby's house is only a few blocks from here. With any luck the Colonel will be there. He'll let me use the phone without making me pass a lie detector test about our relationship.

Five minutes later I'm on Moby's street. There aren't any cars in the driveway, so there might not be anyone home, but I'm running out of options. I cross the Dicks' lawn and pound on the front door. After a short silence, there's the telltale creak of the Colonel coming down the stairs. He jerks the door open and sticks his jaw out. He's wearing army sweatpants, a silver chain, and that's it—unless you count his chest hair that looks like a wool poncho.

I wave hello, trying to avoid focusing on any of the frightening details in front of my eyes. "Colonel."

He looks me up and down. "Chub."

"Were you in the middle of something, sir?"

"Thinkin' about a snack. Why?"

"Can I come in?"

He sticks his head out the door again and scans the street. "Moby's, uh . . . not here."

"Yeah, I know he's out getting coffee or something."

I don't know what's so funny about that, but the Colonel chuckles and a whole bunch of skin that looked pretty solid a minute ago ripples under his hair sweater. "Yeah . . . or something. Well, double time it. I'm sweating like a politician in church out here."

The inside of the house is colder than Lockhart's soul. I put my hands in my pockets and almost flip up my hood when I decide against it. Last time I had my hoodie on in front of him he asked me what I was trying to hide, and then made me say the pledge of allegiance before he'd let me in the house for the next month. I'd prefer a cold head to a sweaty one, anyway.

We make our way into the kitchen. I need to call Margot right away, before the Colonel starts grilling me about what I'm doing there. Once I get the name of whoever bought the stained kangaroo suit, I can kick back, share a snack with the Colonel, and make it home in time for dinner.

I grab the phone off the charger. "Can I use your phone, sir?"

"Checkin' in with HQ, huh?"

"Um, yep."

"All right, but make it quick." He shakes a bag of snacks the size of a pillowcase. "They don't put as much in these bags as they used to. I'm not making any promises."

Moving into the family room, I dial Margot's number from memory. She picks up on the third ring.

"Levi?"

Confused, I check the number on the phone's screen. "No, it's Chub. Do you know Moby?"

"No, but the caller ID says 'Dick,' so I guessed. You really need to get your own phone."

It's hard enough to get my parents to buy me new shoes when my feet outgrow the old ones. The chances of me scoring a cell phone are about as slim as the Colonel making the women's Olympic figure skating team. "Yeah, I'll work on that."

Margot wastes no time on pleasantries. "What do you need me to get for you this time, the *Mona Lisa*?"

"No, this one should be simple."

"I'm all ears."

"I need a name."

There's silence on the line for a minute, then Margot says, "Tired of writing out that alphabet soup of yours on all your assignments, huh? Wish you were John Smith or something?"

"What? Not for me. I need to know who bought the stained kangaroo suit from you last week."

"Oh! Why do you want to know that?"

Years of negotiating with the McQueens has

taught me that the more desperate you appear, the higher the price. The key is to act nonchalant. "Just curious. Nothing major."

"This has something to do with that stupid glass mascot, doesn't it?"

My face gets hot like someone just pointed out my zipper was down in front of the whole class. I could lie, but what's the point? "Yeah. Whoever bought the suit stole the Boogerloo. Can you just tell me who it was?"

There's a sound like she's sucking air between clenched teeth and then she says in a slightly higher pitch than normal, "There are a couple of *teeny* problems with that."

"Such as?"

"One: my services are confidential. If I were to go blabbing about everyone who came to me to get them something, people'd be too embarrassed to ask me for help. My business would dry up like a salted slug."

She has a good point. But maybe there's a way around it. "Could you maybe give me some sort of hint, so you wouldn't have to tell me?"

"Which brings me to issue two: I couldn't tell you who it was, even if I wanted to."

"You didn't recognize them?"

"What, you think I do these deals in person? I'm barely four feet tall! I can't take risks like that."

"How then?"

"I take PayHub. Once I have the money, I tell them where to find the item. Very low risk."

"Who sent you the money on PayHub?"

"Sorry, Chub. It's pretty much anonymous. I prefer it that way. You ever heard the term 'plausible deniability'?"

Less than an hour ago I was sure that this phone call would be the end of it. Now I'm back at square one without a single lead. After thanking Margot for her time, I hang up and flop onto the huge leather sofa. This feels like getting sent back to the beginning in the game Sorry!, only a thousand times worse.

Thankfully, the one person in the world who might be able to help me is right in the next room.

I walk into the kitchen. Before I even put the phone back in the charger, a smell hits me. The Colonel's irritable bowel is probably acting up again. I learned a long time ago that in Moby's family, gassy is a dominant genetic trait. I breathe through my mouth and pull out a chair across from the Colonel.

"So, what have you got on? Your mind?" He's told me and Moby this same joke about three thousand times, so I smile enough not to insult him. His chuckle sends tiny pieces of his snack flying.

"Just asking someone to help me find something."

"I heard something about a bowling ball?"

"Boogerloo," I correct him. "Just something at school that's missing. I'm . . . trying to help them find it."

"Volunteering, huh?"

"Yeah."

He turns the bag toward me, offering me some. I reach in and pull out a puffy little chip. It looks weird, but I'm about to eat it anyway when I suddenly realize that what I smelled when I came in the room was not coming from the Colonel.

"Uh, what kind of chips are these, sir?"

He shoves one in his mouth. "These aren't chips,

220 • MARK MACIEJEWSKI

private. Chips are bad for you. These are pork rinds."

I examine the smelly little glob. If it were possible to 3D print a fart, it would look and smell just like a pork rind. But if there's one thing that being raised by Polish parents has taught me, it's that sometimes weird tastes really good. I pop it into my mouth and the Colonel watches me carefully as I chew. I don't want to insult his snack, especially since he's trying to eat healthy, so I give him a smile and a thumbs-up.

"You know, there's a big difference between missing and stolen," he says.

I'd hoped he hadn't overheard the whole conversation. Normally I'm good at maintaining secrecy, but Lockhart is in my head, and I'm starting to make silly mistakes.

"Who stole what, now?"

He already knows enough. What harm can it do? "Someone stole the school's mascot, and a couple of us are going to get in trouble if we can't prove it wasn't us."

His beard makes a sound like a wire brush as he

rubs his hand on his chin. "How long you been looking for the thief?"

"A couple of days."

He rubs his chin. "What kind of leads do you have?"

"That phone call was the last one. I have no idea what to do now."

"Why not make them come to you?"

What is he talking about?

"Listen, you ever hear about Operation: Tapeworm?"

I rack my brain in case he told us about it before. "I don't think so."

"Of course not! It was top secret."

I grab another pork rind. "That's too bad."

He spins the bag back toward himself and continues. "Well, it happened way back when. I'm sure it's not top secret anymore."

I sit forward in my seat, but not close enough to get hit by any fried pig shrapnel.

"So this arms dealer got his hands on a bunch of bazookas and some other stuff after a certain war, on a certain peninsula." He raises his eyebrows at me.

I nod as though I understand.

"Anyway, he puts the word out that he has this stash and that he's going to sell it to the highest bidder. We had no idea who this guy was, or where he was keeping the stolen stuff. So we came up with a plan to get him to show himself."

Even though the Getter had turned out to be a dead end, I knew coming here was a good move.

"What'd you do?"

"We posed as a rival dealer and put out the word that we'd found his stash and that we were going to steal it."

"Why'd you do that?"

"We were out of moves, and we couldn't let the weapons fall into the wrong hands. It made him panic. He stuck his head up to see who was pinching in on his turf, we figured out who he was, and we grabbed him."

It sounds simple enough. If I can't figure out who the thief is, maybe I can taunt them into making a mistake and showing themselves.

"But you got the weapons back; that's really all that matters."

The Colonel lets out a belch, pats his stomach, and then rolls the top of the bag closed. "We caught the thief, but the weapons were never found. Oh well, you can't win 'em all."

CHAPTER 18

The Colonel lets me make a few more phone calls while I wait for Moby to get home. This time I know he isn't eavesdropping. From upstairs, the Dicks' home theater rattles the whole house, as the Colonel loudly cheers on the whalers during an episode of *Whale Wars*.

I call Sizzler first, since he has a cell phone. He doesn't quite understand the plan, but he agrees to do as I ask and text a couple of people that he heard the thief was caught and that the Boogerloo would be returned tomorrow. Next I call the McQueens, and then Shelby. She doesn't want to come to the phone, and I don't really want her calling my house later when my parents are home, so I tell Grammie I'll just see Shelby on the way to school tomorrow.

I'm about to call it a day when it occurs to me I should probably call the Arch too.

His mom answers the phone.

"May I speak to the—to Archer, please?"

There's a short pause. "Maciek?"

"Yes." It takes me a minute to realize how she knew it was me. She probably doesn't get a lot of phone calls from twelve-year-olds with Polish accents.

"How've you been?" Her voice almost gives my ear a sunburn through the phone.

"I've been . . . well," I lie.

"You haven't been over here in ages."

"Yeah." *Unless you count the time I broke into your son's room a couple of months ago.*

"Well, Archer has been talking about you a lot. It sounds like you boys are hanging out again."

That makes me pause. Just last spring he wouldn't

even act like he knew me; now we're "hanging out"?

"I guess. It's more of a business arrangement for now."

Her laugh sounds like three hiccups followed by a snort. "You are so funny. Well, you are welcome here any time."

"Okay."

Just when it seems the torture of talking to an adult on the phone is over, she says, "And when I see you, I expect all the details on Archer's new girlfriend."

What the heck just happened? I'm pretty sure she just broke about a hundred unspoken laws between parents and kids. And the Arch has a girlfriend?

Girls at Alanmoore have been following him around like a bunch of lovesick puppies since the first day we got there. But there's only one girl I've ever seen him show any kind of interest in. My stomach feels like a water balloon full of worms.

"I don't know anything about that," I say, wishing it were true.

"Oh, okay. Wink, wink." She laughs again. "Oh, here he is."

A second later Archer is on the line. "Hey, Chub. Any luck?"

I fight down the sick feeling and tell him what I need him to do. He agrees, and then we plan to meet in the hallway tomorrow to see if it works.

As soon as I hang up, I dial Megumi's number as fast as I can. I want to tell her the plan before the Arch has a chance to. Her stepmom answers and calls for Megumi. I have plenty of time to wonder what her and the Arch's kids will look like while I wait for her to pick up.

"Sorry about shoving you out the window."

"It's okay. My butt broke the fall." I slap my forehead.

She giggles. "Thank God for butts, huh?"

Most of the blood in my body rushes directly to my face. "Yeah, butts are good." As smooth as I am, I can't believe the Arch is the one with the girlfriend and not me.

I explain the plan to her, and she agrees to help spread the word to the Trondson kids she knows from last year.

"Okay, so we'll all *conveniently* be in the main hall tomorrow before school starts to see who's acting weird. Right?"

"I'll be there."

"Good."

There's another pause, and I think she hung up. Then she says, "I thought you were calling to cancel."

"Cancel what?"

"Emerald Con. This weekend, remember?"

In all the excitement, I'd forgotten about the tickets. But if she still wants to go with me, maybe she isn't the girl Mrs. Norris was talking about after all.

There's about as much chance of me missing Emerald Con as there is of me growing an arm out of my forehead. "Why would I cancel that?"

"You know, because I shoved you . . . and broke your butt."

"Oh, don't worry. It already had a crack in it." I'm glad she can't see how red my face is right now. "I'll see you tomorrow." I hang up before she answers, and before I have the chance to say anything else about my broken butt.

Jarek is coming over for dinner, and I don't want to be late and have to answer a bunch of questions about where I was.

The Colonel lumbers down the stairs as I'm gathering my things to go. He takes a look at me and stops. "You okay? You look like you ate a bad sardine."

I almost ask if there's such a thing as a *good* sardine, but I really don't want to have that discussion right now. My stomach's been upset over the thought of getting expelled. But when Mrs. Norris said the world "girlfriend," for some reason it was like throwing a flare into a pool of gasoline.

"Not feeling well, sir. I think I'll head home."

He flips me a lazy salute. "Understood."

Before the Colonel shuts the door behind me, I turn. "Tell Moby I'll call him later?"

"Roger that."

As I head out toward home, I pray Moby doesn't have too much coffee. If we're going to spot the thief tomorrow, everyone will need a good night's sleep.

Jarek pulls up just as I'm climbing the stairs to our front porch. Normally I know it's him without having to look, since his ancient Acura sounds like two blenders fighting inside of a garbage can. But I don't realize it's him until I hear the trademark screech of his tires as he jerks to a stop. The car sounds different, even though it looks the same. If the car were a dog, it would be time for one last trip to the vet.

My cousin pops out of the car, all smiles. "Not bad, yes?"

"What's wrong with your car?"

He looks offended. "I tuned it."

I thought tuning something made it sound better.

"I wanted it to sound cool."

If the sound of a fart echoing inside of an empty soup can is his idea of cool, he's hit the bull's-eye.

I roll my eyes. "Awesome."

"Do you think?"

"No." The comment might cost me a ride or two, but do I really want to ride around in the dysentery mobile?

He waves off the comment and follows me into the house.

By the smell coming from the kitchen, my mom is making my favorite, Polish stir-fry. *Polish* stir-fry is just like *regular* stir-fry, except instead of fresh veggies cooked in a wok and served with rice, it's Hamburger Helper.

Jarek kisses my mom on the cheek and hands her a red-and-white can.

"What's this, Jarek?"

"You told me to bring vegetables."

My mom examines the can. "These are fried onions."

He puts his palms up and hunches his shoulders. "Yeah, vegetables."

My mom just shakes her head and opens the can. The contents go into the stir-fry, just like whatever else happens to be lying around.

Jarek and I wash our hands and set the table.

"You find the Boogerman yet?"

I shoot him a look to keep his voice down, but my mom probably can't hear us over the sizzling pan of meaty goodness on the stove. "No, but I have a plan."

Jarek chuckles. "I'm sure you do. Just make sure your parents stay bolivious."

I consider correcting him, but I'm pretty sure he says things wrong to make me mad, so I let it go. "I'm always careful. Why would this be any different?"

He shrugs. "Uncle Kasmir just seems more . . . irritable than normal. Plus, they asked me to cover for both of them at the shop tomorrow. Something's up."

I don't like the sound of that. I can't remember a time when at least one of them wasn't there. Jarek is right; something is up if both of them need to be gone at the same time.

My dad gets home just as we finish setting the table. I study him as he drops his briefcase in the living room and takes off his windbreaker. He does look out of sorts, but not the way Jarek described. He kind of looks like a balloon with just a little bit of air let out of it.

My mother says grace, then dishes us all up. My mom's feelings get hurt when I attempt to make her Polish "delicacies" edible by adding ketchup. But for some reason today she doesn't care when I hose down a plate of stir-fry. I turn the bottle upside down over my plate and squeeze it like it owes me money.

When I only have about half the correct amount on top of my meal, my dad suddenly takes the bottle from my hands and sets it on the table out of my reach. "Enough. Ketchup does not grow on trees."

I don't argue, but I do look at my mom out of the corner of my eye. She's shooting my dad the *we'll talk later* look.

Then Jarek discovers something more uncomfortable than silence. "Something bothering you, Uncle Kasmir?"

My dad stops chewing and looks at my cousin. By the look on Jarek's face it's obvious he wishes he'd kept his mouth shut. Does tuning your car make you an idiot, or is it the other way around?

"Nothing for you boys to worry about."

My mom clears her throat to get my dad to look at her, but he's developed a sudden interest in the pattern on his dinner plate. When he still doesn't look up she puts her fork down and says, "Kasmir, they are old enough to talk about these things."

My dad puts his fork down too and rubs his forehead. I really don't think I want to hear whatever it is.

"It is not a big deal. Just things to do with business."

Not satisfied with his explanation, my mom takes over. "Business is slow. If we want to keep up with the competition, we need to take out a loan to get new machines."

Is that all? I was worried it was something really serious.

I can see my dad has said the last he intends to say on the subject.

My cousin, however, is not as perceptive. "But you told me never to borrow from anyone."

My dad's nostrils flare with his breath. At least if he starts breathing fire, it'll hit Jarek and not me. "This is true, but we are not borrowing from anyone. We are borrowing from ourselves."

Jarek gets a quizzical look. I get ready to dive under the table if he makes one more comment to my dad.

Before he can shove his size thirteen foot in his mouth again, my mother interjects. "This is why we need you tomorrow. We need to go to the bank to sign papers on a home equity loan."

Realization dawns on Jarek's face and he nods. "I know this. You borrow money out of your house." He finishes the math in his head. "You borrow from yourself. No way you can lose."

I'm almost not paying attention anymore. My mind is on one thing and one thing only. Tomorrow I have to catch the thief, or else my parents will have to look for a house in a different city when Lockhart drops the axe on me.

My dad has resumed eating and he actually appears relieved that it's all out on the table now. "Almost right," he says. "The only way this goes bad is if we had to sell this house before the loan is paid off. If that happened, we'd have to sell the shop to pay it back."

My mother tries to sprinkle some sunshine on the conversation. "Stop scaring the boys, Kasmir. There are other options."

"True," my dad says. "If we had to, we could always move back to Poland and work for Stanislaus."

Suddenly, a plate of Polish stir-fry covered in a layer of ketchup doesn't look quite as appetizing.

CHAPTER 19

In my dreams last night, me and my parents moved into a refrigerator box behind the Dumpsters at my new school. Not only did I not recognize any of the other students, but I couldn't understand a word they were saying. I stumbled around the place trying desperately to get anyone to talk to me, but they all shoved me away like I had leprosy or something.

Then I realized why no one was responding. I was speaking English and everyone else was speaking Polish.

I'm not sure if my shout when I wake is in real

life, or in the dream. It doesn't matter. The puddle of sweat on my pillow is real. My dad has been itching for a reason to move back to the old country, and if we have to sell the house and move to a different school district because I get kicked out of Alanmoore, he'll have one.

I'd set my alarm for half an hour earlier than normal to make sure I have enough time to get to school and spread the rumor a little more before the first bell that the Boogerloo was going to be returned at lunchtime. But I must be so tired from tossing and turning all night that I hit the snooze button without even realizing I did it.

When I finally open my eyes, I've slept through my half-hour cushion, and almost another hour. I'll barely make it on time if I fly out of bed and sprint the whole way.

I crash through the back doors of school a second before the second bell rings, not *technically* late. Luckily, Mrs. Badalucco is distracted toweling off her chins, which gives me the chance to slide into homeroom unnoticed.

Shelby glances over when she sees me, then quickly looks away. If the disappointment on her face could be weaponized, my parents would buy out her stock.

Moby waves at me, and I shoot him a chin-raise in acknowledgment. The caffeine must still be in his system because he looks a lot more chipper than usual.

Then I owl my neck around to Megumi. She stares back stone-faced for a minute. What kind of mystery infraction did I commit to get her upset? She finally lets me off the hook with a wink.

Mrs. Badalucco starts class by talking about the assassination of Archduke Ferdinand and the start of World War I.

I immediately check out. My mind won't stop playing out scenarios that could happen if I can't figure out who the thief is. Do I run away before my parents can send me away? Do I throw myself on Lockhart's mercy? Do I buy a toupee and join the army?

When I momentarily check back in, Mrs. B has somehow turned the lesson about the war to end all wars into a story about the time she got into a fight with her sister-in-law at her cousin's wedding. I have no clue what she's talking about; I just know the sister-in-law started it.

When class is over, I signal Moby, Megumi, Sizzler, and Shelby to follow me, and then I race to the Arch's locker. The McQueens spot me and join the meet-up.

The Arch looks as tired as I feel, and he gives me a suspicious look. "Where were you this morning, Chub?"

I feel stupid saying I overslept, so I say instead, "I had to handle some last-minute stuff."

"Whatever. Is it on for lunch?"

"I hope so. Did you guys spread the word?" I look around the circle of faces as they all nod. "Good. Then the only thing left to do is be there when the lunch bell rings, wait, and watch."

Moby raises his hand.

"Yes, Mobe."

"What happens to the thief when he gets caught?"

I know exactly what will happen, but I don't want to say it out loud.

"I mean, seriously. Are we talking jail time?"

Megumi shoves his arm playfully. "You're funny. Stop it!"

Moby rubs his arm. "Okay, sorry." He shuffles a few steps away from her.

She laughs and looks at me. "Moby can hang with me."

I nod. I doubt he'll actually be seen hanging out in the hallway with a girl, but at least he won't feel left out. I wish everyone luck and we break it up in time to make it to our second classes before the bell.

When the lunch bell rings, I fly out the door on rubbery legs. I guess I'm more nervous than I thought. I dash to the top of the main staircase, then slow to a normal pace so that I don't attract attention. My propaganda campaign must've worked, because the hall is much more full than normal. I mesh in with the crowd and try to eavesdrop on as many conversations as I can. Maybe it's wishful thinking, but I'm sure I hear the word "booger" a lot more than usual. When I get to the landing where I split my pants earlier in the week, I stop. This is the perfect vantage point for the main hall. Plus, as a bonus, the door to the walkway above the courtyard is right behind me if I need to disappear quickly.

I made sure we'd have the entire area covered. That means spreading everyone out around every entrance to the main hall. The only problem with my spot is I can't see the positions I assigned the others. I have to trust that everyone is where they're supposed to be.

Suddenly there's a commotion under the stairs that I can't see. I crane my neck over the railing. Troy and Marlon from the track team are hopping through the crowd like a pair of overgrown rabbits. Apparently the Arch did his part last night.

"Is it there?" Troy calls, trying to see into the trophy case over everyone's heads.

Marlon, who's taller, stops in front of the case, turns, and throws his arms up. "Negative. We do not have Boogerloo!"

Troy catches up, and they laugh and slap hands before weaving their way out of the hall toward the cafeteria. I scan the kids who witnessed the display of testosterone-fueled buffoonery. No one is acting nervous at all, which makes me start to sweat. Something has to happen. I can't take the fall for this. I close my eyes and say a desperate prayer to whoever is the patron saint of lazy little Polish kids who didn't do it.

When I open them again, the hallway is clearing out—and the Arch is standing next to me.

"What are you doing here? You were supposed to be covering the east hallway."

He rubs his neck. "I got there and Shell-by was already there. She scares me, man. It's the eyes." It's good to hear that I'm not the only one, but I expect improvisations from Moby, not him. "I circled around up here. I figured maybe I'd see something on the way."

"Did you?"

He shakes his head. "Nothing. I think word got around and pretty much everyone who's still in the building was down in the hall by the trophy case."

Except you.

The sound of the door behind us slamming makes us both jump.

He looks embarrassed that it got him too. "Ha, wind."

I turn around to check the door, and spot the thing sitting on the landing. The Arch sees it too and we both take a step closer. It takes me a minute to realize what we are looking at. It's a stuffed kangaroo, like the kind you can win in the claw machine at Thunder Alley Bowling and Fine Dining, but it's covered in something that looks like snot, and it has a piece of paper around its neck. Written on it in big black marker is one word:

WAHOOOOOOOOLIE

"What the heck is that, Archer?"

"Why are you asking me? You're the one who was sitting here."

Then a sound out of a nightmare echoes in the hall.

Lockhart booms, "What are all of you doing in the hall?" She chases after kids, who flee like a flock of sparrows. "We can just as easily have lunchtime after school, if that's what you prefer, Ms. Nickelson!"

I need to get the snotty kangaroo before she sees it. I lunge for it, but the Arch is quicker. I grab it a split second after him.

He grits his teeth. "Let go!"

I grit back. "You let go."

Then the smell hits me, and I instantly realize what's covering the stuffed toy. It's rubber cement, and it's still wet. If he wants it so bad, he can have it. I let go of it, but it won't let go of me.

I look at the Arch and see panic in his eyes. I'm about to tell him to back out the door and we'll figure it out in the courtyard when I hear the sound of heels on the stairs.

Lockhart looks at us like a snake would look at a pair of fat mice with their paws rubber cemented together. "Why don't the three of you come to my office for a little chat?"

In her office, Lockhart makes Mrs. Osborne unstick us from the toy while she makes herself a cup of tea. She sets the sticky, plush glob on a spare file folder on Lockhart's desk, and scurries out of the room, probably not wanting to get splattered by chunks of middle schooler when Lockhart tears us apart.

Me, the Arch, Lockhart, and the toy sit in silence, the fumes from the rubber cement stinging my eyes.

"That's funny." She laughs, but there's no happiness in it. "I get it, you know. The rubber cement . . . it looks like nasal effluvium."

I almost laugh too, but not for the reason she thinks.

"Did either of you ever stop to think why I haven't issued any discipline for the theft yet?"

Even though she didn't read us our rights, we both elect to stay quiet.

"It was because I had no evidence, only suspicions." She stands up and paces behind her desk. "But now that you choose to make this into a joke, you've forced my hand."

I want to wipe the sweat forming on my forehead, but my hands are still covered in rubber cement.

"Do either of you want to tell me anything?"

I want to tell her a lot of things, but I don't think any of them will make this any better. The only positive is that technically she still doesn't have any proof, but since she caught us sticky-handed, I doubt she will really care.

"Nothing?" She picks up the file folder with the snotty toy on it. "This is going to cost you." With a sweep of her arm she flings the stuffed kangaroo at the trash can, but it misses and hits the wall instead. The rubber cement sticks and it hangs off the wall like a big, purple loogie.

We both choke back giggles.

"I'm glad you think it's funny. Maybe you'll think this is funny too."

I look at the Arch out of the corner of my eye. He is trying not to look at the kangaroo slowly walking down the wall.

"If the Wahoolie isn't back by the end of the school day Monday, you are *both* expelled."

CHAPTER 20

"What!" the Arch and I cry out in unison, which barely gets a raised eyebrow out of Lockhart.

I'm too stunned to say anything else, but thankfully, the Arch isn't.

"You can't just go around throwing kids out of school without any evidence!"

Lockhart looks at him like she can't believe he's serious. Then she reaches into her desk and pulls out the single largest file I've ever seen. When she drops it on the desk it makes a *whoomp* like the subwoofer in

Jarek's car. I don't think I want to know what's in a file that dense.

A cocky grin crosses her lips. "Even principals as incompetent as Shelly Mayer keep detailed files of all disciplinary actions."

My stomach drops like a runaway elevator. I'd always banked on Mr. Mayer's incompetence. This is not good news.

She strips off the jumbo rubber band that's holding the file together and opens it. She reads from one of the pages. "Arson." She looks at us like she's impressed. "You two have quite a colorful past."

I take a deep breath to keep my voice from shaking. "That was an accident. Mr. Mayer knew that."

"Mr. Mayer had things on his mind other than doing paperwork for the school. Bringing disciplinary action against a student would have invited a lot of unwelcome attention. Thankfully, I have no such . . . preoccupation." She flips over the stapled bundle that must be the arson case.

I flick my eyes to the stupid little mug she loves to show off. I want to say, *What about your boyfriend?*

She peruses the next packet, and then flips through several more of them, scanning the headlines. "Stealing a mascot, attempting to poison the track team . . . what *haven't* you two gotten into?"

Nothing comes to mind immediately. My face is hot and tight like an overcooked kielbasa. This isn't fair.

"So, as you can see, I have all the *evidence* I need."

"None of those things happened this year," I blurt out.

"Perhaps not, but a fire alarm was pulled yesterday. If someone—oh, say, the principal—had witnessed that—"

The Arch shifts forward in his seat. "You weren't even here when—"

My hand flies to my forehead, but I disguise the move by using it to rub my brow instead. Realizing how stupid his outburst was, the Arch slumps in his chair.

She gives him an amused look, and then her eyes narrow. "All you need to remember is that unless the . . . item is returned in one piece, it will be the words of a pair of arsonists against one of the most respected *educators* in this or any other state." The word "educator" comes out sounding like Professor Snape.

She reassembles our file and replaces the rubber band. With a heave, she drops it back in the desk drawer. When she looks up again she seems surprised we are still there.

"That is all. I will see you both on Monday."

The end-of-lunch bell rings just as we leave the office, so we quickly plan to meet after school. I'm going to need a couple of hours of uninterrupted thinking time to figure out what we are going to do. Thankfully, I have language arts next, then algebra.

In language arts we're making the outlines for stories that we will be writing later in the quarter. I wasn't listening when Mrs. Sigurdson explained how to do an outline, so hopefully one looks something like the matrix I sketch out in my notebook of all the facts in the case. By the end of class all I have are the names of everyone I can imagine having the nerve to take the stupid thing. I draw a line through the one name I know for sure didn't do it, my own.

The final bell rings at the end of algebra. Normally getting out on Friday of the first week of school would be one of the best feelings a kid can experience (my dad would say "a job well done" is right up there). But today it's the starting gun in a race against my own destruction. Lockhart is right; if she decides to throw us out, I should just consider myself thrown. Nobody would take Archer's and my word over hers, least of all my parents. Maybe it's an immigrant thing, but they think anyone in a position of authority walks on water. If Jarek is right about my dad itching for a reason to move back to Poland, Lockhart is about to hand him one.

After a summer of tai chi and self-reflection, I'd come back to school less than five days ago determined to stay away from the type of trouble I'd always sought out in the past. How could things have gone so wrong, so fast?

After the final bell I avoid the halls by going one flight up to the library, then out the secret door and down the abandoned staircase. It's raining when I open the door from the basement into the parking lot. Apparently even the sky has decided to dump on me today. I move close to the building to avoid a complete soaking, and when none of the kids waiting for the bus are looking, I slip through the gap between the Dumpsters. The McQueens, Shelby, Megumi, and Moby are already there. The Arch slips in a few seconds after me.

One of the McQueens pulls out a hat and puts it on. When it's adjusted to the proper angle, he nods approvingly. "Decided to poke the dragon, eh? The McQueens approve."

"What are you talking about?"

"The bit with the snotty toy. Brilliant!"

Before I can reply Megumi jumps in. "It wasn't them. Lockhart smelled rubber cement in the hall during fifth period. She searched Danny Moles's locker and found half a jar."

The McQueens trade a knowing look. "Probable cause," the hatted one says.

Moby raises his hand and the Arch scoffs. Moby puts his hand down. "Who's Danny Moles?"

"He's the one who named the Boogerloo. Remember, at the assembly?" Megumi says.

Actually I made up the name. Danny was just the one dumb enough to say it loud enough so Lockhart could hear. Realization hits like someone dumped a cup of ice water down my back. *Of course, Danny Moles!*

I shoot a glance at the Arch. His eyes widen when he puts it together. "Danny Moles, duh." He runs a hand through his hair and laughs. "We're off the hook."

Shelby clears her throat. "Ahem, there are two small problems with your theory." She looks around to make sure she has everyone's attention. "One, Danny is an idiot. There's no way he planned and executed a heist of that sophistication. It's simply impossible."

She's right. Danny is the kid who missed a couple of days last year after eating a jar of habañero peppers in an attempt to give himself a fever to get out of standardized testing.

Moby goes to raise his hand again, then stuffs it in his pocket instead. "Maybe he's only *pretending* to be an idiot."

The Arch slowly turns and gives Moby a sideways look.

Shelby clears her throat again. "Which brings me to my second point. Remember the assembly where he yelled out and got in trouble?"

We all nod.

Shelby looks at us like she can't believe she has to spell it out. "Don't you see? It couldn't have been Danny. He was in detention when the Boogerloo was stolen. He's literally the only one who has an alibi."

For a moment no one speaks, then the McQueen pipes up. "So what's the play, Chub?"

Everyone is looking at me, and I have absolutely no idea what to tell them. I'm learning new things about having a Cadre all the time. For example, having one makes it really easy to disappoint everyone you care about all at the same time when you're in way over your head and have no clue what to do next.

"I need some time to think about this."

"Dude!" the Arch says. "Were you not listening to Lockhart? We don't *have* time."

Megumi flattens her eyebrows in concern. "What does that mean?"

I look at the Arch, who makes an ushering motion

with his hands. "It means if the Boogerloo isn't returned by Monday, we're toast."

Shelby's hands go to her mouth and she gasps. The McQueens shake their heads. Moby looks like he wants to disappear.

Megumi just looks mad. "But you didn't take it. She can't do that."

The Arch looks like he did when Moby took him out at the poker tournament last year.

Megumi sees him sulking and pats his arm. Seeing her comforting him makes my scalp burn. But it cools down a few degrees when I remember that I'll be the one going with her to Emerald Con tomorrow. At least I'll get to do something cool before my life comes to an end Monday. I suppose if I was granted a last wish, it'd probably involve Emerald Con and reading *Ronin Girl* anyway.

"She saw me go into the school right before it disappeared. She can blame whoever she wants for the fire alarm. It's her word against ours," I say.

Shelby wrings her hands. "We have to find it. That's all there is to it."

I throw up my hands. "I'm open to suggestions."

"I . . . *you're* the mastermind."

Right now I don't feel like the master of anything. "Just stay as close to the phone as you can. I'll think of something." Everyone nods, then picks up their bags to head home in the rain.

I reach down and heave my bag onto my shoulder. When I turn to go Shelby is blocking my way. For a split second I think I'm about to get the soul-stare, but she has a totally different look in her eyes.

"What will happen if you get kicked out of Alanmoore?"

This time I avoid her gaze for a different reason. I don't want her to see how scared I am. "I'll think of something," I say.

I hope I'm right.

One by one everyone slips out of the alcove and disappears. After Shelby leaves, Megumi is next. Before she goes she turns and does the pinky-thumb-telephone sign that she'll call me later to plan our trip to Emerald Con in the morning.

Finally, it's just me, Moby, and the Arch. The Arch

kicks a pebble with his shoe and watches it ping off the recycling Dumpster. "Last weekend of freedom, huh?"

"I hope not."

The Arch laughs. He looks at Moby, then at me. "Listen, Chub. I just want you to know . . ." He doesn't finish.

But I think I know what he was going to say, because I feel the same way. Even though the circumstances suck, in a weird way it's been kinda fun getting in trouble together again.

Moby lets out his breath in a whoosh. "What? What do you want him to know?"

The Arch shakes his head. "Never mind. I'll see you guys tomorrow."

I almost correct him and tell him that I have plans tomorrow, but I don't want to have to explain that I'm going with Megumi, so I just nod. Quick as a rabbit, he turns and disappears through the gap.

CHAPTER 21

The last thing I need right now is to get drafted into dry cleaning service by my parents, so we head to Moby's house. The rain turns Moby's linen shirt see-through, and he spends half the walk dropping his backpack because he's trying to use his arms to hide his nipples.

I don't mind the rain. When it's raining, nobody can tell if you're sweating.

We're greeted by the smell of pizza rolls when we get there. We drop our wet things in the entryway and head to the kitchen. The Colonel is just sliding what looks like an entire box of the little bundles of pizza-flavored goodness onto a platter. He's wearing an apron that says NO, YOU CAN'T HAVE IT "WELL DONE."

He licks his fingers. "Men."

"Colonel."

"You boys are good soldiers. Did you manage to keep your powder dry?"

Moby shrugs. "I don't use powder anymore, Grandpa." He turns to me and whispers louder than a freight train, "Gave me a rash in my armpits." He flaps his arms like a penguin to make sure I get it. "Plus—"

The Colonel holds up a hand to stop him. "Uh-uh! What's the number one rule between two men who share a bathroom?"

Moby recites rule one. "Don't ask, don't tell."

"Atta kid." He offers us the platter, and we both grab handfuls. Then the Colonel whisks away the tray and heads upstairs. Moby and I wait until we hear him flop into one of the chairs in the theater room before taking our snacks up to his room. He makes me wait in the hall while he changes out of his wet shirt.

When he lets me in, we get to work on our snack.

For a few minutes the only sound in the room is Moby's chewing. He shakes me out of my thoughts when he says, "What will your parents do if you get kicked out of Alanmoore?"

"I don't know. I guess we'll have to move."

"Man, that sucks."

That's the understatement of the year. "I'm a survivor, Moby. I'll be fine."

He raises his eyebrows. "I wasn't talking about you! What am I supposed to do if you have to go to a different school?"

"I don't know. The same thing you always do, I guess."

Desperation crosses his face. "Chub, *I* hang around with *you*. That's what I do."

I guess I never considered it from his point of view. He's right; he will be lost at Alanmoore without me. The thought of him wandering the halls alone makes my stomach feel like it's falling through a trapdoor out my butt.

But what can I do? I've played every angle I have, and none of them has led me any closer to catching whoever stole the stupid thing. I'd love to tell him that I've got a plan to get me—I mean us—out of this, but I don't want to lie. I can't even look him in the eye. I bet no one has ever looked so sad while eating pizza rolls before. I pop one of the little lava pillows in my mouth and choke it down, along with the realization that I am letting down not only Moby, but the rest of the Cadre too.

My parents are gone when I get home. There's a note on the fridge from my mom telling me that they'll be late at the shop getting ready for tomorrow, and there's dinner in the fridge for me when I get hungry. I'm still pretty stuffed with pizza rolls, but I could eat again, if properly tempted. There's a plastic wrap–covered plate in the fridge. Dinner consists of three pieces of fried Spam (delicacy), some green beans out of a can, and a puddle of pudding. I think my mom plans meals by doing Internet searches for pictures of TV dinners.

I take the Spam, bite one bean in half, spit it into the sink, and leave the bitten piece on the plate along with a smear of pudding, then I shove the rest down the disposal so my mom isn't insulted when she gets home.

After that I grab the phone and call Megumi.

"You ready for tomorrow?" she says as soon as she answers.

"I think so."

"You don't sound very excited."

I picture Moby earlier, sadly chewing his pizza roll. "I have a lot on my mind." She doesn't reply. "So what's the plan?" I go over to the desk in the corner of the kitchen and fire up the Compusaurus, what I call our ancient computer, to browse the schedule for Emerald Con while we talk.

"Do you remember where I live?"

How could I forget? "I remember."

"Well, why don't you come here in the morning and we can walk together?"

Most of the Emerald Con page has loaded. Nothing in particular catches my eye, but just as I'm about to give up, a name pops into view.

Tatsuo Kobayashi will be making a rare personal appearance. And the better news is that he'll be signing autographs.

"Okay!" I say a little too enthusiastically.

"Great. Because I have a surprise for you."

Part of me wants to tell her that I already know her dad will be signing *Ronin Girl*, but she's excited to tell me herself, so I don't let on that I already know.

When I hear my dad's car bounce and scrape into the driveway, I quickly say good-bye, switch off the Compusaurus, and fly upstairs. I don't want to get cornered, in case he changed his mind about not having me work tomorrow. As always, I have a backup story prepared about a surprise project I have due Monday, just in case.

The next morning, I shoot out of bed, wide awake before my feet hit the floor. I put on the button-down shirt I wear when I help Jarek at the theater, but I have my League of Honor shirt underneath. I wait until it sounds like my parents are finishing their morning coffee before I make my appearance in the kitchen.

My mother makes me a two-minute egg with little strips of toast to dip in it. Just as I'm dunking my first piece into the yolk she kisses me on the head.

"Good-bye, *rodzynek*. Have a good day."

"Work hard," my father says, downing the last of his coffee.

The second the car's bumper scrapes the driveway, I dump the rest of my breakfast and fly out the door to meet Megumi.

All the walls around Maplehurst look exactly the same. At first I think I might be searching the wrong one, but after a few minutes I find the hole behind the leaves.

I can't explain it, but I feel weird walking right up to those giant doors and ringing the bell. Maybe it's because the only other building I've ever been in that has doors that tall is our church.

Megumi opens the door, all smiles. Her shirt has a picture of a cartoon mouse lying in a field of daisies with a pink samurai sword stuck in his chest.

She notices me looking and glances down. "It's a statement. Do you get it?"

I do not. "Yep."

She bops my arm playfully. "Too good, right?"

"Almost."

She laughs, then picks up the backpack propped

against the wall and heaves it onto her shoulders. "Let's roll."

Emerald Con is at the convention center downtown. It isn't far, and thankfully, the entire walk there is downhill. Even if Kobayashi isn't the best father, I don't want to be all sweaty when I meet him.

We spend the first couple of minutes of the walk talking about comics and movies. I thought I knew a lot about rare comics, but Megumi knows about ones I've never even heard of. I commit as many of the names to memory as possible so I can look them up later on the Compusaurus.

When the convention center comes into view, Megumi is quiet.

"Are you okay?"

"Yeah, I . . . thanks for coming with me today," she says.

Why is she thanking me? "No problem."

She laughs, and it makes me feel like I'm missing something obvious. "I mean, thanks for everything." My confusion must show on my face because she says, "You know, letting me be a member of your Cadre and everything. I never had friends like that at my other schools."

Joining the Cadre this week was about as lucky as getting the last ticket on the *Titanic*.

"I'm the one who should be thanking you. I would've never been able to go to this if you hadn't invited me." She shrugs it off like it's no big deal. "Seriously, I have an appointment with the executioner Monday. I'm pretty much looking at this as my last request before the axe drops."

She laughs and playfully swats my arm. "Wow. Dramatic. I'm sure you'll think of something." But her eyes tell me she doesn't believe what she's saying.

When we get to the convention center, I step into the line of people waiting to walk through security. Megumi veers away and signals me to follow her.

I weave my way down the sidewalk after her. There's a big sculpture on the corner that looks like a soup bowl with gigantic blades of grass growing out of it. When I emerge from the crowd on the sidewalk, she's sitting on the rim of the bowl. "I found your Wahoolie," she says.

At first I'm confused, but then the sun hits one of the things coming out of the sculpture and I see it's made of glass. I search the ground until I find a small plaque embedded in the sidewalk. It's a Wahoolie, all right. I could do without the reminder right now.

"What are you doing up there?"

She beams. "This is the rendezvous spot."

"Who are we rendezvousing with?"

She doesn't have to answer, because just then a familiar-looking SUV pulls up to the curb and Moby hops out. He's wearing a set of Superman pajamas that I haven't seen him wear in three years. His stepmom rolls down the window and waves.

"Hi, Maciek!"

I'm not sure if it's the fact that Megumi invited him without telling me, or that his pj's are so small they look like they are made of body paint that makes me unable to respond. A horn blares behind his stepmom and she takes off with another wave.

Moby shuffles over to me. He's even wearing the matching red Super Slippers that go with the pj's. "Hey, Chub."

"Hey, Mobe. What are you doing here?"

"Megumi invited me. Where is she?"

Megumi drops from the sculpture and sticks a perfect superhero landing between us. "Surprise!"

She studies my face and the smile disappears from hers. "What? I thought you'd want to have all your friends here."

Normally she'd be right, but I thought it was just going to be me and her and *Ronin Girl.* I don't want Moby to feel awkward, so I change the subject. "Why are you wearing pajamas?"

He looks himself over. "It's co-splay."

I slap my forehead. "I think you mean *cos-play.*"

"I think he looks awesome," Megumi says. "Are you making a statement about how comics let us stay kids forever?"

That is definitely not what he's doing.

Moby nods. "Um, yeah."

Megumi lifts the cape attached to the back of his shoulders, fluttering it like he's flying. "You are too funny." She fishes in her pocket and pulls out the ticket envelope, handing one to each of us. There's still one left in the envelope.

I'm about to ask her if she got an extra ticket by mistake when the Arch steps out of the crowd wearing a Wolverine T-shirt. When she sees him, her smile gets even wider.

CHAPTER 22

"Awkward" does not begin to describe what it's like with all of us standing in line together. What I'd hoped would be a chance for Megumi and me to bond over our mutual love of rare comics is now the world's weirdest pajama party.

Megumi slides up next to me. I can tell she senses my tension. "Were you surprised?"

I try to sound happy. "You could say that."

She looks down. "You're mad, huh?"

The question catches me off guard. *Am I mad?* "No, I just thought . . . I guess I thought it was going to be just us."

Her eyebrows shoot up. "You always have your friends around. I thought you liked it that way."

I glance back at Moby standing next to the Arch. She doesn't know the whole story. I guess I can't be too mad at her for assuming the Arch and I are actual friends. Then something else occurs to me. "You didn't invite Shelby?"

"I did, actually. She had something she had to do with her Grammie this weekend."

I don't want it to get any more awkward than it is. "Thanks for inviting them. You didn't have to do that."

She takes a deep breath. "I didn't exactly do it one hundred percent for you."

Great. Here's the part where she tells me she'd rather read *Ronin Girl* with the Arch than with me. "Okay?"

She thinks for a minute before she says, "My dad doesn't even notice me. All he thinks about is stupid *Ronin Girl*. So I'm going to talk to him here, where he can't ignore me. I figured it would be easier with my friends around."

There's one huge flaw in her plan. If she embarrasses him, and he thinks we put her up to it, the chances of him signing anything for us will be drastically reduced. I'm about to ask her if she's sure this is what she wants to do when she nudges me on the shoulder.

"I'm sorry to put you through this."

Even though she doesn't show it, I bet she's supernervous. And when I'm supernervous, nothing makes me feel confident like knowing my Cadre has my back.

But then I think about her huge smile when she saw the Arch, and my head starts to sweat. I'm not surprised she likes him. Pretty much every girl at Alanmoore thinks he's the greatest thing since Wi-Fi. But why does *he* have to like the one girl who might have a chance of understanding who I really am? Is that something a true friend would do? I'm so busy asking myself that question a thousand different ways that I barely notice Megumi splitting off into the bag check line. When I look up again I'm walking through the metal detector and through the doors.

When I'm finally inside and get my first look

around, I want to fall to my knees and weep. The hall is jammed with people dressed as their favorite characters from comics, video games, and movies. Some of the costumes look homemade, like the guy in the green sweats with the paper-mache Ninja Turtle shell on his back. Some of them look straight-up movie quality. One lady is dressed like Pikachu, but her leotard has a huge tear right in the middle of her chest. At least Moby's pajamas aren't the most embarrassing outfit here. As I take inventory, I'm actually starting to kick myself for not wearing a costume. I'm about to take off my jacket and the shirt covering my League of Honor tee, when an old-school Cylon walks by me and glances down.

"Check out Mini Me!"

The guy next to him, Undead Super Mario, turns and looks. "Naw, that's Lex Luthor."

The Cylon nods, impressed. "Way to commit, kid." He rubs a hand over his own chrome dome.

At school that comment would've meant something entirely different than it means here. Here, it's a compliment. These are my people.

Even though she's the smallest of the four of us, Megumi leads us through the crowd like the only scout with a compass. We find a spot out of the flow of traffic and circle up to discuss our plans.

Apparently, Megumi is the only one not dumbstruck. "What do you guys want to see while you're here?"

I'm here to meet Kobayashi, so I let someone else go first.

After we all glance around at each other, the Arch raises his shoulders. "I want to check out the League of Honor booth."

That makes me pause. "Me too."

Megumi checks out the map and taps the LOH booth. "Okay. Moby?"

The look on his face makes it obvious which "booth" he needs to visit first. I quickly scan the perimeter of the room and find what he's looking for.

After fifteen minutes of waiting for Moby to *coach the Browns to the Super Bowl*, we are all ready to take on Emerald Con. Kobayashi's signing starts at noon. That leaves us forty-five minutes of free time if we want to get in line an hour early.

The League of Honor booth is everything I hoped it would be and more. Pretty much every issue of the comic is available to buy, as well as collectibles and some props they used in the movies. There's even an actor dressed in the actual costume of Doctor Truth. It wasn't the same guy who played him, but that doesn't make a difference to me. It costs ten dollars to get your picture taken with him, so I act like I'm not interested as the Arch and Megumi jump in line. Seeing them giggle as they wait behind the rope barricade makes my stomach flop, but it does a full seizure when Megumi says something to Doctor Truth and he hands her the most powerful weapon in the League of Honor universe, the Lance of Knowing. I should be the one holding the Lance of Knowing, or at least the one up there posing with Megumi.

When they're done with their photo shoot we regroup and check the time. We need to head over now if we want to get a good spot in line. The closer we get to where Kobayashi will be signing, the tougher it gets to maneuver through the crowd. I get slapped in the face by several tails and one huge foam sword before we make it to where the line begins.

Megumi, who's been leading the way, turns around. She has a nervous smile on her face. "Well, here we go."

I turn to make sure we're all still together. The Arch is right behind me, but Moby is nowhere in sight.

"Archer, where's Moby?"

"He was right behind me a minute ago."

I scan the area again, looking for a pair of Superman jammies that are stretched to their limit. Megumi already has one foot in the line.

"He's fine, Chub. He's probably in the bathroom again."

With Moby, aftershocks are not uncommon, but neither is disappearing when he gets nervous. I take another glance at the forming line. The couple of seconds I've spent looking around has already cost us a lot of space.

I look at Megumi again. Her face pleads for my decision.

The Arch makes an ushering move at us. "You

guys go. I'll find Moby and meet you on the other side."

Before I can tell him to check the men's room first, Megumi has me by the wrist and we are surfing a wave of her dad's fans through the rope barricades. We end up pretty far back, behind a girl dressed like a samurai. She's holding a vase in one arm and a copy of *Ronin Girl* in the other. The vase looks just like the one they put my Uncle Stosh's ashes in after the funeral. Maybe she's bringing her uncle to Emerald Con one last time.

After a few minutes of silently creeping forward in line, I decide I better say something to break the tension.

"I guess your dad's more famous than I thought."

"Yeah, he's a big deal." She looks around at the crowd and sighs. "Do you think this is stupid?"

As someone who spends most of his time trying to avoid being noticed by his parents, trying to get yours to pay *more* attention to you does strike me as odd, but I keep that to myself. "I don't think it's stupid. I think it's actually pretty brave."

She smiles and stands up straighter. "I'm sorry to put you through this." When I don't respond she puts her hand on my arm just like I saw her do to the Arch. The touch makes my legs feel like a stack of blocks that will topple if I try to move them. "And I promise, as soon as this is over, we'll sit down and read *Ronin Girl.*"

If I'm not on a slow boat to Eastern Europe.

At exactly noon a murmur runs through the crowd. The curtain behind the signing table rustles, then parts, and Kobayashi steps through. The murmur erupts into cheers. People draw their homemade samurai swords in salute.

The line moves slower than Moby's insides that week he didn't eat anything but red meat and peanut butter. After an eternity we reach the merchandise table near the front of the line. The guy behind the table looks like a bean bag with eyes. A ring of fuzz that looks like a chinstrap for a nonexistent helmet sprouts from his third chin. "Kobayashi will sign one item." He motions to the collection of graphic novels and comics fanned out on the table. "Choose wisely."

I quickly scan the inventory and pick up a sleeved copy of *Ronin Girl* in English.

Neckbeard puts his hands up like I'm handling a live bomb. "Please be careful with that."

I ignore him and flip it over, trying to look casual as I check the price. I almost drop it when I see the number. "One hundred dollars!" The end of the word "dollars" comes out as an embarrassing squeak.

"Sir, that is a *Ronin Girl* number one, which will only become more valuable. I cannot imagine a better investment. I would, however, recommend asking Mr. Kobayashi to sign the sleeve so as to preserve the mint condition of the piece itself."

I take a look at the cover one more time and then set it down. I can't afford that kind of investment.

Megumi moves over next to me. She fishes in her bag and pulls out her Japanese copy. When neckbeard realizes what she's holding, he gasps like a five-year-old who just spotted a unicorn. She waves it around casually, meaning to tease him, but making my stomach flutter too. "I'll get him to sign this one for you. I know where to get more."

A gap has opened in front of us, so we hustle to catch up, and before I know it, we are next in line. We watch as the girl in front of us proudly introduces Kobayashi to her dead uncle. He smiles a polite smile and makes small talk with her for a moment before she rolls up her sleeve and he signs his name on her biceps. She bows deeply to him before bounding away toward the exit.

The lady in charge of the line pulls back the rope, letting us through. My legs are rubbery as I walk toward the table. Megumi holds onto my arm again, but this time I'm not sure who's helping who.

Kobayashi is reaching under the table when we get there. He comes up with a water bottle and opens it without looking up. Without hesitation Megumi drops the comic on the table. Kobayashi recognizes it and the corner of his lip curls in a small smile. Then he raises his head and sees who is standing in front of him.

His smile disappears when Megumi speaks. "Hi, Dad."

He looks at me, then back at her. "Megumi?"

She takes in a deep breath and says the words she has no doubt been rehearsing. "You're always busy at home. Is this a good time?"

Kobayashi's eyes flash, but he must realize everyone is watching him, so he forces a calm look back onto his face. After a deep breath he folds his hands and says something in Japanese.

Megumi shakes her head. "This *is* the time and place. Besides"—she turns around and raises her voice enough for the people in line to hear—"I waited in line. I should get as much time as anyone else."

Kobayashi smiles slyly. He whispers something to the assistant beside him and stands. A muted "booo" floats through the line.

Megumi folds her arms. "Where are you going?"

He smiles, but it's meant for the crowd, not for her. "Not here."

Before I know what's happening, they both disappear behind the curtain. The line lady comes over and gently pushes me toward the exit. I don't resist, but as soon as she turns around I slip back under the ropes. I sneak along the curtain until I'm behind the stage where Kobayashi was signing autographs. No one can see me here, so I move along the curtain looking for a gap. When I finally find one I stick my head through it.

Instead of the luxury dressing room I'd imagined, the backstage is cluttered with crates and supplies. In the corner there's a table. Kobayashi and Megumi sit on folding chairs at one end of the table, facing each other. He does not look happy.

They speak quietly in Japanese, but no matter what language, there's no mistaking a good old-fashioned parent lecture. Megumi looks sad at first, but when it's her turn to speak she sits up straight and looks her father in the eye.

He listens, taking in her words. But then she pauses, picking at a fingernail nervously. When she speaks again she doesn't say much, but whatever she says makes her dad fume. He looks away from her.

Then he's back in lecture mode, and her resolve is gone. He keeps lecturing for a few more minutes, but it loses intensity as Megumi shrinks down in her chair. Suddenly the look on his face changes. He stands and walks around to her side of the table. Then he kneels down and puts his arms around her. After a moment she puts her arms around him too.

I'm about to close up the curtain so I can be by the exit when she comes out, when a hand clamps down on my shoulder.

CHAPTER 23

I'm yanked backward out of the curtain like a mouse being dragged from its hole by the tail. I knew Emerald Con was too good to last. I didn't get to meet Kobayashi, and I couldn't afford to buy anything anyway. Why not top it all off by being tossed out by security? But when I spin around to face my judgment, it isn't neckbeard like I expect; it's Moby and the Arch.

The Arch looks at me like I'm crazy. "What are you doing?"

I catch my breath and explain what I just witnessed behind the curtain.

"Wait, her dad wrote *Ronin Girl*?"

"Yep."

He shakes his head. "Wow, that's pretty cool."

I guess so, but I think I'd rather have parents who care about me, even if they show it by making me work all weekend doing jobs it would be illegal to make a kid do if he wasn't related to you.

The crowd still waiting to meet Kobayashi lets out a collective "booo!" We race around the corner to see what's happening. The cattle chute of ropes is emptying. The faces of the people drifting away all show the same thing: disappointment.

I stop a girl dressed like a stormtrooper. "What happened?"

She pulls off her helmet. "They just came out and said that Kobayashi had an emergency and wouldn't be signing any more autographs. I can't believe I missed him."

I thank her, then scan the crowd. Megumi comes bounding out of the mass of people, a huge smile on her face.

"I saw your dad yelling at you. What happened?"

She's grinning, but her eyes look like she wants to apologize. "My dad canceled the rest of the appearance. We're going to go talk right now."

Even though he's just disappointed a conference hall full of geeks, he's made the one geek that matters very happy. I'm glad for Megumi, even though nothing today has worked out the way I'd hoped. I guess I should just consider it practice for the rest of my life. It's hard enough being the weird foreign kid at Alanmoore. But at least I've sort of figured out a way to fit in, at least within the Cadre. If I end up back in Poland, I'll be a double foreigner (if there's any such thing).

"So, I'll see you guys at school?"

I look at the Arch. He doesn't seem like he wants to think about Monday morning any more than I do. "Yep, see you there."

With a small wave, Megumi slips off behind the curtain and disappears, leaving the three of us standing alone.

The Arch breaks the silence. "So, what else do you guys want to do while we're here?"

Now that the excitement has died down I feel the weight of Monday morning lying on me like a dead walrus.

"I think I want to go home," I say.

The Arch nods. "Yeah." Apparently he feels the walrus too.

Without another word, the three of us find an exit and start walking up the hill toward home. The Arch finds a pebble and kicks it up the sidewalk, so I know he has something on his mind. Finally, he comes out with it.

"Megumi's pretty cool, huh?"

"Yeah!" Moby says, startling me. I'd almost forgotten he was there.

The Arch laughs, then looks at me for my answer.

Maybe if I don't elaborate he won't realize how cool she really is, and he'll lose interest. "She's cool," I say.

But he doesn't let it drop. "Do you like her?"

I feel my pulse in my scalp. "Why would you ask that?"

"Well, you have been hanging around with her."

Technically she's been hanging around with me, but I let it go. "I mean, you just went to Emerald Con with her."

"So did you."

"I know. But you didn't know we were coming. Besides, I'm not the one getting all defensive about it."

I stop walking. "Well maybe you don't have anything to get defensive about."

He kicks the pebble into the street, where a passing car promptly runs it over. "What's that supposed to mean?"

Moby is directly in between us. If he had an uncomfortability meter on his head, it would be in the red.

Before I can stop myself the words are spewing out of my mouth. "It means you obviously know I like her. So why are you trying to like her too?"

He huffs. "I don't know. She's cool."

"There are plenty of cool girls at Alanmoore."

He stuffs his hands in his pockets. "Fine. I like that she doesn't know about all the messed-up stuff I did last year. She likes the new Archer, or I guess I mean the old Archer. You know what I mean. Not 'the Arch.'"

I know what he means. Megumi didn't know me before, either. She likes me for who I am now.

He goes on. "What makes you think you have some kind of exclusive on her anyway?"

Moby backs up and does his best to blend into the brick wall behind him.

I throw my hands up. "Seriously, what do you have in common with her? She's got taste; you're wearing a Wolverine shirt. Do I really need to do the math for you?"

The Arch winces. That punch landed. Then he hits me with one of his own. "You gave me this shirt for my birthday. I wore it as a peace offering. I thought you'd think it was cool."

Now I remember. I gave it to him back in second grade.

"I mean, didn't you think it was weird how small it is on me?"

"I think it fits you good," Moby says, then glances at me. "I mean *well*." He throws me a wink that looks like he got poison ivy on his eyeball.

I take a deep breath. The next words are hard to say. "Archer, everything is easier for you than it is for me. Can't you just leave Megumi alone?"

He jams his hands in his pockets and looks at the skyline of the city with a thousand-yard stare. "It doesn't work that way, Chub."

"What, is that some sort of threat?"

"It means you can't just plot and scheme your way to what you want all the time. One of these days it's going to catch up to you."

"When, Monday?"

He shrugs, and the look on his face turns cold and cocky. I'm not looking at Archer any more; I'm looking at the Arch. "Let's just put it this way: if one of us is at a different school, I guess this little issue is resolved."

My stomach feels like it's been impaled on an icicle. He doesn't say another word, just turns and walks off down a side street.

What the heck just happened? Has he been playing me all along, pretending to be my friend so I wouldn't suspect him, only to throw me under the bus in front of Lockhart? After what he just said, I'm positive he is the thief. The only question is how do I prove it to Lockhart?

"What a jerk," I mutter to myself.

"I think you're both being jerks," Moby says. Then he turns and walks toward his house.

My parents are going to lose our house and their shop because of me. A feeling like hot acid rises in my throat, just like when I looked in the mirror and saw my bald head for the first time. Maybe it's guilt, or maybe I just want to start conditioning myself to my new life of hard labor, but I decide all that's left for me to do is to walk to my parents' shop and throw myself on *the Pile*.

When I get there, as usual, my mother is happy to see me.

My dad gives me a suspicious look. "Did Jarek fire you?"

I'd forgotten I was supposed to be helping at the theater. Thinking quickly, I say, "No, I just did too good of a job. Got done early." Before he can ask any questions I say, "I figured I'd get a head start on *the Pile* before it gets too deep."

My dad gives me the suspicious look again, then nods slowly. "Good thinking," he says, and then he goes back to bagging up a rack of freshly pressed shirts.

The Pile is a mountain of donated clothes that we clean and delouse before handing them out to local shelters. I guess I don't have to tell you that people rarely donate really nice clothes. Therefore, the pile smells like the combined BO of about a hundred people. Once, during detention in the library, I searched "Worst smell in the world" on Mrs. Belfry's computer. The top result was something called "Stinky Whale Syndrome," which affects one in ten whales. I've never personally gotten a whiff of SWS, but I can't imagine it's any worse than *the Pile* at the end of a long summer. I've never tried the prepunishment-to-buy-mercy strategy before, but hopefully, this is bad enough to work.

I work the rest of Saturday, then Sunday morning. Sunday afternoon, I hear my parents arguing at the front of the shop. A minute later my dad comes to the back where I'm working. He rubs his neck.

"You need to go outside."

At first I don't know what he means, but then I

connect the dots. They were arguing about me spending the whole weekend in the shop. My mom won, like she usually does, and my dad got to come tell me. At least one of them feels sorry for me.

"Home by seven," I hear him say as the heavy steel back door to the shop closes behind me, and I hold my hand up against the blinding sun. That gives me a couple of hours to go make things right with at least one person.

Ten minutes later I'm ringing the Dicks' bell. Moby's dad opens the door. "Maciek!"

I flinch when he shoves his hand at me, then brace myself for the inevitable crushing my hand's about to receive. "Mr—" He raises an eyebrow. "Jason."

He pumps my arm like a well handle. "Cool, cool."

His definition of "cool" is crushing people's hands like they're crackers he's about to put in soup. As soon as he lets up the pressure, I yank my hand back.

"They're upstairs." He points with a thumb. "Tell them I just made a batch of kale chips if they have the munchies."

I already know what the Colonel will say, and feeding Moby kale would be like throwing a water balloon full of gas into a campfire, so I will not be mentioning it. "Will do," I say, then bolt up the stairs before he tries to get me to go to vegan CrossFit or something.

Moby and the Colonel are in the theater room. A football game is on the TV that takes up almost an entire wall.

"Private," the Colonel says when he sees me. Moby glances at me for a second, then looks right back at the screen.

"Sir. Who's winning?"

"I'll tell you who's not winning—the fans." Moby rolls his eyes. Apparently he's heard this one before. "So many rules; now it's basically just a bunch of grown men playing tag."

I look at the screen just in time to see a player get hit so hard his helmet flies off onto the sideline.

"When I was a kid, concussions were good for you."

"They were?"

He fumbles with the remote, finds the right button, and changes the channel. "Sure! I think . . . it was a long time ago."

Usually the Colonel has some nugget of wisdom when I need help, but today I don't think even he can help me. The most important thing I can do right now is make things right with Moby before the world falls apart tomorrow.

"Moby, can I talk to you?"

Moby grabs the lifeline I've just tossed him and jumps up out of his seat. When we're in his room he lets out a deep breath. "Thanks. He gets pretty fired up watching football. He was almost to the part where he claims drinking water is for sissies."

Before there's a chance for an awkward silence I blurt out what I have to say. "I'm sorry about yesterday."

Moby sits on his bed and tries to cross his legs. When his jeans refuse to yield after several grunting attempts, he gives up and settles for crossing his ankles instead. "Why are you so mad at the Arch? I thought you guys were becoming friends again."

"I thought so too."

"Are you mad he was there yesterday?"

"I don't know. Kind of."

Moby looks out the window. "Are you mad I was there?"

"What? No!"

"Okay, good."

Now the silence I was avoiding happens. After a minute Moby says, "You think he stole the Boogerloo, huh?"

I nod. "I've gone over this a million times. It's the only thing that makes sense. He's been pretending to be my friend so I wouldn't suspect him. Now that Lockhart's ready to pounce, all he has to do is set me up, and he's got his revenge for us taking him down last year."

"I don't know, Chub. You're the mastermind and all, but I'm the one who actually took him out at the poker tournament, and he was pretty cool to me. I got lost yesterday, and he's the one who found me."

I'd meant to ask him about that before he stormed off. "Where the heck were you, anyway?"

"Well, since you might be moving away and everything, I wanted to get you something. You know, like a going-away present. I saw it and stopped to look, and when I looked up you guys were gone."

I swallow hard. The thought of him getting me a going-away present makes it feel like I'm as good as gone. "What was it?"

"Well, I was going to wait until you were leaving for sure, but . . ." He goes to his desk drawer and pulls something out. "Maybe we can check it out together while you're still here."

Moby isn't the best gift giver, so I prepare myself to look grateful for whatever it is.

When he turns around and holds out the gift to me I don't have to pretend anything. There in his hands is a sleeved, mint condition, Japanese language copy of *Ronin Girl*.

"What?" is all I can manage to say.

"It's that comic, right? The one Megumi has."

My mouth is dry and my butt feels like it's stapled to the chair. "What?"

He pushes it toward me, and I take it with a shaking hand. "Is that the right one?"

I stare, taking in every detail. "It's the one," I manage to say. I flip it over and examine the back cover, afraid to take it out of the sleeve. Then I remember the price tag. "How did you even get this?"

Moby takes a deep breath. "Well, it was expensive, and I know you guys are poor, so I called my mom. She talked to the guy and used her PayHub to buy it. It was easy."

I'm so in awe that I have my own copy that I don't question him. None of my relatives would ever get me a gift this good, but if they did, my mom would make me hug them. I don't want it to get weird, so I just say, "Thanks, Mobe."

He beams with pride. "Only problem is they didn't have it in English. I'm not sure what language that is. It's not Polish, is it?"

"No, this is the original. It's written in Japanese."

Moby's shoulders sag. "Oh—"

"What's written in Japanese?" The Colonel's voice from the open door makes us both jump. For a senior citizen with bad knees he's pretty good at appearing out of nowhere.

"Nothing, Grandpa. Just a comic book."

The Colonel steps into the room. "Let's have a look." I hand it to him and I'm relieved that he treats it with the proper reverence. He squints at the cover for a second, then pushes up his lower lip, impressed. "*Ronin Girl*, huh?"

I stare at the Colonel in shock. "How do you know that?"

He points at the lettering. "Says it right here."

My mind struggles to catch up. "Wait . . ."

But Moby says it before I can form the words. "You can read Japanese?"

The Colonel looks offended by the question. "Course I can. Spent eight years on Okinawa. I used to own a—well, an establishment there."

A quick glance at Moby tells me he hasn't figured out what has to happen next.

"Colonel, is there any chance you'd read that to us?"

He looks at the book again. "It is almost nap o'clock."

"Please!" Moby and I both say in unison.

"All right, but I want to put my feet up."

A minute later we are settled in the theater room. The Colonel is reclining in his favorite chair, and me and Moby are in position over his shoulders so we can see all the panels as he reads.

He skips some stuff he doesn't think is important, and I have to remind him to translate absolutely everything. He seems especially annoyed waiting for us to soak in all the drawings before flipping the page. Ronin Girl's story is a maze of deceit and split loyalties, not unlike my own.

As he reads, my mind wanders to what's in store for me tomorrow morning. I play back the past week in my head, sorting through all the details for the one clue that will confirm what I now know. By the time the Colonel flips the last page, I don't need to go over it anymore. I'm more convinced than ever of exactly who the thief is.

And, as he has so many times before, the Colonel has come through for the Cadre without even realizing it.

CHAPTER 24

The next morning, I meet Moby at the corner way earlier than usual. I need to be at school before the thief to make sure they aren't setting up a double cross. I can't come this close only to get framed because I overslept.

"Did you stick to the plan last night, Mobe?"

He sighs. "Yeah. I haven't had anything to eat since lunch yesterday. Should be calm seas all morning."

I asked him to skip dinner the night before so he wouldn't be hit with any sudden urges when I might need him the most.

We stop a block away and peek around the corner

of the building across the street from Alanmoore. The parking lot is deserted. There won't be anyone there but teachers and the janitor for at least half an hour. It's raining again, so I nudge Moby forward and we make our final approach. Running into Lockhart now could kill any hope of being able to confront the thief, so we press ourselves against the building and quickly move toward the door that leads down into the custodian's basement office and the abandoned stairwell. My plan is to be hidden across from the thief's locker so I can look inside when the door is open.

Moby and I slip through the unlocked door to the basement, and up the abandoned staircase. When we are through the library and safe in the fourth-floor hallway, we let out deep breaths. Moby also lets out something else.

He helps me fan it away. "Oh, man. Was your mouth open?"

I squint to keep it from stinging my eyes. "It's okay." Moby did not inherit the Colonel's nerves of steel.

The hall clock tells us we still have about twenty

minutes before students start to arrive. Plenty of time to stow our bags in our lockers and get into position. We creep down the main stairs to the third floor. With no students in the halls, Alanmoore is an echo chamber. We don't drop our guard until we're in the alcove where our lockers are. I spin the lock as quietly as I can and ease up the handle to avoid the signature *ka-chunk* of a forty-year-old steel locker popping open. I'm about to take my bag off my shoulder to stow it when something falls out of the locker and hits my foot.

I bend down and pick up the folded note off the floor. My hand is shaking as I open it and read the block-printed words:

DUMPSTERS. IT'S OVER.

Someone got up even earlier than me.

I'm too impatient to go back the way we came, so we take our chances with the back stairs. When we get to the ground floor and open the doors out to the parking lot my heart is hammering. I ignore the cold rain hitting my scalp as I march toward the Dumpsters, ready to finish this once and for all. When we get to the opening between the Dumpsters I stop to make sure Moby is still with me. He gives me a quick nod, and we go in.

Someone else is already there. Standing in the thin beam of gray morning light is the Arch. On the ground in front of him is the Boogerloo.

"Chub?"

"Archer." I try to sound cool, but my stupid voice cracks at the end.

Moby tries to snap his fingers. "I knew it!"

The Arch gives him an annoyed look before focusing on me again. "I didn't—" the Arch starts to say.

I wave a hand, cutting him off.

"Don't bother. This is over."

He chuffs out a defeated breath. "Yeah, so the note said. And I see you brought a witness to say you caught me with it."

"I'm not going to lie; that would be a pretty good plan, except for one problem."

"What problem?"

"The only way that plan would work is if I was the thief. And I've told you a million times: I. Didn't.

Steal it." I give him the supercool look I practiced in the mirror last night.

He leans away from me. "Stop looking at me like that. It's weird." Then he points a finger in the air. "Well, the same goes for me. The only way I could've framed you would've been if I had stolen it, and then had my own witness here."

There are whispers and shuffling in the gap between the Dumpsters, and my heart revs like a chain saw. Are those his witnesses?

But a second later Shelby, Sizzler, and the McQueens appear in the tiny space. When they see me and the Arch squared off, they all freeze and stare at us, trying to figure out what they've just walked in on.

Sizzler breaks up the awkward silence. "What's going on, guys?"

One of the McQueens rifles through his brother's messenger bag. He finds the hat he's looking for and stuffs it on his sopping head. "Sweet juggling Buddha!" He points at the Boogerloo.

Shelby rubs a finger on the inside of her wet glasses and squints at it. "No way!" She spins to face the Arch.

He instinctively puts up his hands to shield himself from her inquisition glare. "I didn't do it!"

She gives him the stare for a minute, then straightens the hem of her sweater and wags her finger at the two of us. "You know what I think? I think you two deserve each other."

The Arch and I look at each other, confused. Then he folds his arms. "I'm not taking the fall for this."

"Neither one of us will be taking the fall for this," I say. "Isn't that right, Megumi?"

Everyone looks around, then back at me like I'm losing my mind. For a minute I think I might've been completely wrong. I don't have to wait too long to see that I wasn't.

There's a gasp as Megumi appears out of the deepest shadow in the back of the alcove. "How did you figure it out?"

As coolly as I can, I reach into my bag and pull out my copy of *Ronin Girl*. When she sees it, defeat washes over her face. "I read a great story last night. It's about an orphan girl who becomes a samurai. But then she decides that rather than use her skills to serve the evil

Empress, she'll use them to steal from the rich and give to the poor. But the best part is the end."

Megumi lets out a deep breath.

"That's where she fights off a swarm of samurai to reclaim a very special item stolen from a farmer by the Empress. When she returns it to the farmer he transforms back into the noble samurai he was before it was stolen and he had to leave his daughter at the orphanage."

"The farmer was her dad," Moby says. "It took me a while to get it too."

The Arch gulps. "What was the thing—the thing she brought back to him?"

I fix my eyes on Megumi. "That was the final piece of the puzzle. It was a vase. But not just any vase; the finest one in Japan. Moby's grandpa thinks the vase symbolized the farmer's honor, which was stolen from him. But I think it's the Boogerloo."

I've never spiked a football, but if I had one, I'd spike it right now. I look around at the faces of the Cadre. They all look either shocked or confused.

"I knew it!" Moby says.

My eyes are locked on Megumi. She looks smaller than ever, like she wants to crumple in on herself like a piece of paper.

"My dad's whole life is about *Ronin Girl*. I guess I thought if I did the things she did, maybe he'd pay attention to me, too."

The hunch I had as the Colonel read to us last night was right. "Only instead of stealing a vase, you stole the most valuable thing you could find."

Realization spreads on the Arch's face. "You had it in the backpack at Emerald Con."

She smiles. "Go big, right? I figured if the Boogerloo was worth enough, he'd either be impressed or freak out. Either way, he'd definitely notice me."

"Well, which was it?" Sizzler asks.

Megumi looks up. "Neither one, really. He just got all serious and then we sorta . . . talked. I swear I was just going to show it to my dad at Emerald Con, then return it. I wasn't going to get you guys in trouble."

I level my eyes at her. "You're cutting it a little close, aren't you?"

Megumi makes a cheesy smile and shrugs.

The Arch raises his hand. "So, how do we return this thing without Lockhart thinking we took it in the first place?"

Everybody looks at me.

My first thought is that we could all smuggle it in, wipe our fingerprints off it, and put it back in the case like nothing happened. If we get it in the case before Lockhart catches us, we can call the whole thing a prank and maybe get detention at the worst. I can live with that.

Then Shelby clears her throat. "Guys—"

But Megumi interrupts her. "*I'm* taking it back." She reaches down and picks it up off the ground. "I did this. I'm not letting any of you take the fall for it. My dad understands me now. If I get in trouble with Lockhart, it'll be okay."

The Arch clears his throat. "Wait a second. I thought the whole point of having a . . . um . . ." He sweeps his hand around.

"Cadre," Sizzler says.

". . . Cadre, was to stick together." He walks over

and takes the Boogerloo from Megumi. She looks stunned at first, but then a smile spreads on her face. My stomach drops. I solved this case, why should he get to swoop in and be the hero at the last minute?

"He's right." I grab it too. "We can figure out how to put it back."

The Arch pulls on the Boogerloo. "What are you doing, Chub?"

"I'm being a good friend," I say through gritted teeth.

"No you're not! You're trying to be a hero."

"Why should you get to carry it for her?"

"Guys!" Shelby says even louder this time. Neither of us take our hands off it, but we stop struggling and look at her. "There's something I need to tell you."

As I'm distracted, the Arch yanks the Boogerloo out of my grasp. I scrabble for it but the only thing I can wrap my fingers around is the electrical cord hanging off the bottom of it. We make eye contact for a second, each of us telepathically ordering the other to let go. The Arch has a good grip on it, but as he gives it one more yank his foot slips and he falls backward into the recycling Dumpster with a loud *gong*. The Boogerloo slips from his hands.

For a moment it hangs in the air.

Then it falls to the ground and explodes into a million tiny pieces.

No one speaks. We just stare at the shattered mess. I glance around the alcove. The only person who looks me in the eye is Shelby. She's about to say something, but before she can, she's interrupted by the last sound any of us wants to hear.

Lockhart's voice booms in the tiny space. "It looks like I'll be needing more expulsion forms than I thought."

We all sit in Lockhart's office in stunned silence. The only sound is the growl of Moby's empty stomach like a distant whale song. His guts are pretty active when he isn't under any stress; I shudder to think what's happening in there now. We all jump when Mr. Kraley drops a garbage bag containing the remains of the Boogerloo on Lockhart's desk.

She looks at the bag, then at each of us with a

glare that could extinguish the sun. "The school district brought me here to clean up the mess that Mr. Mayer left behind. I thought getting rid of one or two troublemakers would do the trick." She looks directly at me, then the Arch when she says this. "It always has in the past. But now I see the problems here are much deeper than just a few bad apples. It looks like I've inherited a . . ." She waves her hand around looking for the right word.

"Cadre?" Moby offers.

She narrows her eyes. "A crime syndicate." She stands, walks to the cabinet in the corner, and puts hot water and a tea bag into her little mug. She sits again and takes a sip of the steaming tea. "Do any of you have anything to say before I start filling out paperwork and calling your parents?"

I lean forward in my chair, but before I can speak Shelby says, "I have something I'd like to say."

An amused look appears on Lockhart's face. "Yes, Miss Larkin."

"Shelby—" I try to stop her, but she ignores me.

Shelby shoves her glasses up on her nose. "Well, since you asked. I think there's—"

"I did it." Megumi says. "Nobody helped me; they didn't even know I was doing it. For the last week they've all been trying to catch the real thief."

Like well-trained actors, everyone puts on their best innocent victim faces. Everyone except Shelby.

She looks like Megumi stole her line. "Yeah, but—"

Lockhart gives Shelby her own version of the inquisition stare. "Now might be a good time to keep your mouth shut and let Miss Kobayashi finish her confession."

Shelby ignores her, then cocks her head. "Your mug; is that a Wahoolie?"

The corner of Lockhart's eye twitches. "Why do you ask?"

Shelby folds her arms over her chest. "I think you might want everyone else to wait outside for a minute."

CHAPTER 25

None of us speak as we wait in the outer office. After the longest five minutes of my life, Lockhart's door sweeps open. I stand up, fully expecting to be called in so she can finish the inquisition. But it's not Lockhart who opens the door. Instead, Shelby steps through it, a huge smile on her face.

"Thank you, Ms. Lockhart," she says.

I look at her for some sort of clue as to what the heck is happening, but the smug smile isn't going anywhere. Then it feels like the temperature drops twenty degrees, and when I look, Lockhart fills the doorway. I'm not positive, but I think the crooked crack between her lips might be her own version of a smile.

"Miss Kobayashi, will you step into my office for a moment." It isn't a question.

I flop back down in my seat to wait my turn.

Megumi slides past Lockhart and into the office. But instead of closing the door behind her, Lockhart pauses and looks at the rest of us. "Shouldn't you all be getting to class?" The first bell of the day rings just as her door clicks shut.

The halls are almost empty by the time we get our tardy passes from Mrs. Osborne and leave the office. We head toward the stairs in a loose pack. The passes mean there's no hurry to get to homeroom, but we walk fast anyway, trying to get as far away from the office as possible. The second bell rings, leaving the halls abandoned except for us. When we get to the stairs I've had as much of Shelby's silence as I can take.

"What the heck was that all about?"

She looks shocked. "Still haven't learned not to be nosy, have you, Maciek?"

316 • MARK MACIEJEWSKI

There's no way I'm leaving it alone. Instead I do my best to conjure my own version of her soul stare.

Shelby laughs. "You're doing it wrong." Then she walks up a few steps above the rest of us and turns around. "But since you're all so eager . . ."

The Arch lets out an annoyed sigh. "Is she always like this?" The rest of us nod.

Shelby ignores us. "Ask yourselves this: Did any of you really think that blob of glass was good enough to be a priceless piece of art?" No one answers; we know it will just draw it out even longer if we do. "Well, it smelled fishy to me, so while the rest of you were busy going to comic fest, or whatever, on Saturday I decided to do something useful. I got my Grammie to take me to the Wahoolie gallery downtown." She has our attention and she's loving every second of it. "He was there!"

"Who?" Moby says.

Shelby looks like she wants to pop with pride. "Wahoolie! I met him." The human flamingo is in full flap; she won't require any more prodding. "I told him what a dump this place is, and how the school can never afford anything, so the mascot he made for us really meant a lot. The only problem was he had no idea what I was talking about." She pauses again, giving us time to do the math. "It was a fake!"

"I knew it!" Moby says.

The sight of the Boogerloo hanging in the air before shattering on the ground flashes in my mind.

The Arch runs a hand through his hair, confusion twisting his face. "How?"

Shelby folds her arms. "Apparently, Ms. Lockhart bought some private glassblowing lessons with Wahoolie at a charity auction last year. During the lessons she made the Boogerloo herself. He said she also made herself a teacup."

I run it through in my head. "So he's not even her boyfriend?"

Now the smug smile is back. "Well, not yet."

The Arch loses his patience. "What do you mean 'not yet'?"

"That's what I was telling her when you guys were waiting outside. Wahoolie was so moved by my description of Alanmoore that he wants to make us a real Boogerloo. But that's not all. Believe it or not, he remembered Lockhart. And here's the really weird part: he told me he liked her." I force back a gag. "He's going to invite her back to help him make it." She does one more dramatic pause. "Of course, I didn't tell her *that* part until she agreed to only give Megumi in-school suspension for a week. Oh, and I almost forgot." She fishes in her bag and pulls out a crumpled piece of fabric we all recognize. "I made her throw this in too." She hands the closest McQueen the hat.

Darwin, I think, puts it on his head, but he doesn't say a word. Instead, all three of them take turns giving Shelby hugs of gratitude.

I could probably give her a hug too, but there are too many people around for that, so I pat her shoulder instead. I'm trying to think of a way to apologize for the way I treated her, but she sees the look on my face and stops me.

"I know, Maciek. You're welcome."

At the second-floor landing Sizzler and the McQueens say good-bye, then head off for their homerooms. Moby, Shelby, the Arch, and I stand in the bricked-off landing by my locker.

"I can't believe it's over," the Arch says.

I'm afraid to let myself believe it. I turn to him. "I'm sorry."

"For what?"

"For thinking it was you."

He laughs. "I can't blame you. I was *sure* it was you."

Moby clears his throat. "Well, I thought it was both of you."

Shelby folds her arms and cocks her hip. "Hello? Did anyone think it was me?"

"No," we all say in unison.

After school Sizzler, Shelby, the Arch, and I meet at the Dumpsters. The rain is over, and the warm sun reminds us that it's been less than a week since summer ended. Normally I'd either be in detention or walking home with Moby right now. I'd been so sure I was going to take the fall that I hadn't even bothered to imagine life after school today. "So, what are you guys going to do?" I ask.

Sizzler jams his hands in his pockets like he has something to say but doesn't know if he should.

Shelby gives him a concerned look. "What is it, Julius?"

"Nothing . . . I mean, I didn't want to say anything but I'm . . ." His voice drops an octave, almost too quiet to hear. "I'm taking singing lessons. My mom signed me up."

Shelby lights up. "Where are your lessons?"

"The music shop on twelfth. I need to get going. She'll be mad if I'm late."

Shelby pushes up her glasses. "I know where that is. I can walk with you."

When he smiles, it reveals braces that look like he recently used them to grate a block of cheese. "Okay."

"Do you know anything about musical theater?" Shelby asks as the two of them head off together.

The Arch watches them go, shaking his head. "I guess everyone's full of surprises. Speaking of which, where's Moby?"

I quickly scan the parking lot. "I don't know. He's usually here by now. Probably needed to make a pit stop."

The Arch sucks air through gritted teeth. "Yikes." We both laugh.

"What's so funny?" Moby says. When I turn, he's standing there with Megumi.

"So, I heard you only got a week of ISS?" I say.

She looks down and nods. "I'm really sorry. I hope you know I never meant to get you guys in trouble."

I don't know what to say to her. I understand that when you have something you need to make right, sometimes you just have to do what you have to do.

The Arch isn't short on words. "Hey, you've got a Cadre now. Maybe next time let us in on the plot from the beginning."

Megumi giggles. "I promise, I will from now on."

I laugh awkwardly, trying to think of something clever to say too. When nothing comes to me I say, "Are you guys ready to get out of here?"

"Actually," Moby says, "Megumi and I are going to go . . . what are we going to do?"

She giggles and pats his arm. "I don't know. Do you like coffee?"

Moby's eyes go wide. "I'll just have water." He

shoulders his gigantic backpack, then turns to me. "Remember, tomorrow's the first Tuesday of the month."

Realization hits me like a bucket of ice water. "Tell the Colonel I'll be there."

The Arch raises an eyebrow. "Who's the Colonel?"

I'm not quick enough to stop Moby. "My grandpa. Chub trims his toenails once a month." Megumi and the Arch grimace. I slap my forehead. "It's Chub's payback for making me beat you in the poker tournament last year."

The Arch doubles over with laughter. "You guys are weird, do you know that?"

Moby nods. "We know." He turns to go and Megumi turns with him. "See you guys tomorrow." The Arch and I watch them until they disappear around the fence at the end of the parking lot.

The Arch sucks in a breath and blows it out loudly. "I gotta admit, I did not see that coming. I thought it would be one of us walking out of here with Megumi."

I nod. "I think I got so mad because I knew she would choose you."

"Yeah, but you had the whole comic book angle, so I was pretty sure she would choose you."

That makes my head sweat. "I guess we were both wrong about just about everything."

"So can we officially call this thing over?" He sticks out his hand, and for a moment I only stare at it.

When I finally shake it, I feel something like a knot unraveling inside of me. "Done."

He puts his hands on his hips and surveys the empty parking lot. "So, what do we do now?"

We start walking. I don't have to think too long before I know exactly what we should do. "Have you ever done tai chi?"

ACKNOWLEDGMENTS

I'll never be able to adequately express my gratitude to every single person in my writing family, but I'm going to try. The Papercuts: Maggie, Kayla (who named this book before it was even written), Jason, David, Cindy, Angie, and my smokin'-hot wife, Donna. You guys are the best thing to happen to Thursday since Thanksgiving. My kids: Max, Elena, Bethany, and Sophia. Super agent Sarah Davies. My wonderful, patient editor, Amy Cloud, publisher Mara Anastas, art director Laura DiSiena, managing editor Rebecca Vitkus, Julie Doebler in production, copy editor Beth Adelman, and all of the sales and marketing people at Aladdin who work so hard to turn ideas into real-life books. Dan Widdowson for another great cover illustration. And my friend Tronds, who gives his life for literature every day.

A huge thank you to my friends at SCBWI and PNWA, as well as all the teachers, librarians, and assorted book heroes out there who actually put books in the hands of kids. You make a huge difference!

Thanks to God for putting all of these amazing

people, and too many other blessings to count, in my life. I hope you are enjoying my dad's company as much as we all did while he was down here.

Finally, I want to thank you. Yeah, you, holding this book right now. Thanks for letting me and my imaginary friends spend a little bit of time with you. Keep your nose in a book. Nobody ever got sent to work on their uncle's potato farm for reading too much.

TURN THE PAGE FOR A PEEK
AT CHUB'S FIRST ADVENTURE:

Once, in front of pretty much the whole school, Moby cut a fart so loud it sounded like a phone book being ripped in half.

I was there. It changed my life.

Moby never even acknowledged it. He just walked away like nothing happened, but the rest of us who weren't already dying of laughter were left to perish from cheddar-flavored colon-gas poisoning. Cutting a gigantic fart in a crowded cafeteria is the kind of thing that can change your whole destiny, but Moby couldn't have cared less. I knew right then we'd be best friends.

My name is Maciek Trzebiatowski. Don't worry,

you don't need to remember how to spell it. It's pronounced "Maw-check Chub-a-tess-key," but people call me Chub because that's the sound "Trzeb" makes in Polish. With a name like that, I know there's no chance I'll ever be one of the popular kids, but don't lose any sleep. I'm over it.

Moby and I don't want to be popular anyway. As far as I can tell, popularity doesn't mean much of anything outside the walls of school. What Moby and I want is to show everyone that the popular kid isn't everything he seems to be.

If we end up becoming infamous in the process, I guess that's a form of popularity I wouldn't mind.

I know what you're asking yourself. Why bother? Why not just blend in like all the rest of the unpopular kids until one day you become the popular kid's boss?

Why? Because when you are a bald sixth grader with a little bit of a Polish accent, blending in isn't an option. When you throw in the fact that the guy who used to be my best friend is now the king of the popular crowd and won't even admit he knows me—let's just say I have my reasons.

Who is this jerk? You know the kid everyone treats like a superhero. He goes to your school; he goes to *every* school. He is a foot taller than everyone by fifth grade. His name is usually Steve or Troy, always one syllable for some reason. At my school his name is Archer Norris, but a couple of years ago, when he became the star of the basketball team, he started calling himself the Arch, and it stuck. When you're *that* kid, the things you say and do don't have to make sense; kids will copy you, just hoping some of your popularity will rub off on them. It's sad, but you know it's true.

Anyway, just because these freaks are taller, better-looking, and more athletic and have hair (more on that later) doesn't mean they should be the only ones who get to say how life works in middle school. The fact that their bodies have no sense of timing doesn't mean they're the superheroes everyone makes them out to be, which is where Moby and I come in. Every hero needs a villain, so we've made it our business to expose the Arch as the ordinary sixth-grade mortal that I know he is. And I'm here to tell you, business is booming.

Batman once said something like, "Light is defined by the shadow it casts." Archer "the Arch" Norris is the sun at the center of the Alanmoore Middle School solar system; Moby and me, we're the shadows.

School is back in session after spring break. I use the back door by the Dumpsters so I can hit the back stairs instead of using the crowded main hallway. The hallway is torture for me, and I avoid it at all costs. It's difficult for people to pick on you in front of a teacher during class. But in the hallway it's the law of the jungle. In the halls popular kids are like pumas, and I'm like a sloth with asthma and a limp. Something is always trying to take a bite out of my butt.

The stone halls of the ancient building are chilly after sitting empty for a week, and the fumes from cleaning chemicals burn my eyes. Apparently, our janitor, Mr. Kraley, didn't get the week off like we did. The place might look like an old asylum, but it smells new. I bet the smell makes most people think of clean places. The smell of chemicals just makes me miss my hair.

Everyone is buzzing after a week off school. I have to turn sideways to slide past a clump of giggling girls.

One of them says "Hawaii" and I try not to think about the five days I just spent at my parents' dry cleaning shop while my classmates were apparently jetting around the globe. I worked on my "character" while they worked on their tans.

A group of guys from the track team are gathered on the landing. I could turn around and take the long way to my locker, but they are so distracted high-fiving one another, I can probably slide past unnoticed. I flip up the hood of my sweatshirt, turtle my head as low as I can on my shoulders, and try to sneak by without any comments.

I'm safely by them when one whips my hood off my head.

"Look, it's Yoda!" he says.

"Bald, he is," another one chimes in. The rest of the jocks crack up, even though he sounds more like Miss Piggy than Yoda.

I want to explain to them that Yoda is actually a Jedi Master and could easily destroy all of them before they even knew what happened, but something tells me that would only make things worse. So I keep walking.

Me and Moby's lockers are in a bricked-up, dead-end hallway that used to be part of an old stairwell leading from the basement to the library about a hundred years ago. It's a nice spot because it keeps us out of the main hallway. I quickly scan the area to make sure no one sees what I keep in my locker, then I open it and dig through my stack of supplies.

I save anything and everything I can possibly use in a future plot to embarrass the Arch. I haven't pulled a prank against him since I propped a gallon of expired milk against the inside of his locker door two weeks ago, and I'm dying to get back to work. I still have a few copies of the eighth-grade health class childbirth video *Wondrous Womb from Whence We Came*. I swapped one for the sixth-grade *Grammar Is Groovy* DVD. Most people wouldn't guess that someone as cool as the Arch faints at the mere sound of the word "biology," but it's true. I was hoping he'd watch the video by accident and pass out. Unfortunately, he was home sick the day the class sat down to learn the proper use of semicolons or whatever and got to witness the miracle of birth instead. A couple of the boys, including a few jocks, cried a little. But without Archer fainting, I couldn't call that particular prank a success. I consider running the videos over to Ms. Harper's room for another try, but I seriously doubt I could get away with it twice. Nothing else catches my eye.

Moby arrives and digs in his locker a few doors down from mine. It looks like he's searching for books, but I know he's just trying to avoid eye contact with other students.

"You want to come over and finish *Watchmen* tonight?" I ask.

Moby has to read the *good* comics at my house because his parents think they'll turn him into a drooling murderer.

Moby shuts his locker, shoulders his enormous backpack, and sighs. "I can't."

"But you only have, like, fifty pages left!"

His shoulders slump. "I got TD tonight."

Moby's grandfather lives with them. He's a retired army colonel and believes in keeping a tight personal grooming schedule. The Colonel is pretty cool—he unwittingly gives us many of our best ideas for messing with the Arch. The only problem is he can't bend down and reach his own feet to trim his toenails, so Moby has to do it for him. As the lowest-ranking member of the Dick family, Moby draws toenail detail once a month. He spends a lot of time praying his parents will have another child so he can get out of it.

"Has it been a month already?" I ask.

He doesn't answer. He doesn't have to. He shudders like a dog that's about to throw up, and I change the subject.

"Jarek was over last night," I say.

He perks up a bit. "Did they get a new movie?"

My cousin Jarek runs the local movie theater, the Clairemont—an ancient movie house that still uses old-fashioned film projectors.

"One came in yesterday. He'll have it spliced and ready for us to watch it Wednesday after school."

"It's not another classic, is it?"

Ever since I convinced him to watch *Spartacus* last summer, he gets suspicious when he doesn't know what the new movie is.

"Don't worry, new release."

He turns to me, his eyes burning the side of my face. "I hope so. *Spartacus* didn't make any sense."

I'm tired of trying to explain the famous scene where all the slaves claim to be Spartacus so the Romans can't tell which one really is.

Moby won't let it go. "I mean, seriously, how can they *all* be Spartacus? That's a pretty big mess-up, if you ask me."

"Mmm-hmm," I say, hoping he'll drop it.

He doesn't. "And if there's more than one, shouldn't the movie be called *Sparta-CI*?" He taps his temple. "Think about it."

I don't need to think about it. "Don't worry, I promise this one is not a classic."

"Is it age appropriate?"

"I think it's about owls trying to save the world or something."

"Sounds lame, but my parents should be okay with it." Moby's parents make sure the movies he watches are "age appropriate," which seriously limits our options.

Moby shuts his locker and grabs my arm. "Wait! Did they get it?"

I shake my head. The "it" he's asking about is the first trailer for the new *League of Honor* movie that's coming out this summer. We've already decided it's our favorite movie of all time, despite the fact that nobody has even seen a single frame of the film yet. Jarek has promised to tell me the second it arrives.

Just thinking about *League of Honor* appears to wipe the Colonel's ancient, yellow toenails from his mind. He doesn't smile exactly, but I know it lifted his spirits.

Jarek has to watch every film before showing it to a real audience to make sure he's put the film strips together right. We get to watch the movies the day before they're released. I would probably eat a bag of hair to see movies before they are released. There's something supercool about knowing things nobody else knows.

We're about to start planning snacks for our latest private premiere when we hear Shelby behind us.

"What's happening Wednesday after school?" Shelby Larkin asks. Her voice stops us cold.

We've been here too long and she's found us. I glance at Moby without turning around. His eyes plead with me.

"Nothing, Shelby. Moby is gonna come over and read the last fifty pages of *Watchmen*." I try to look busy in my locker.

"Hmm. Will that be before or after you watch the new movie at the Clairemont?"

My scalp flushes. I shut my locker and turn to face her.

If someone figured out how to genetically splice an eleven-year-old girl with a flamingo, Shelby would be the result. All her clothes are from thrift stores and smell like funeral parlors and old perfume. Today she has a sweater buttoned around her neck, but her arms aren't in the sleeves. Shelby has been trying to get invited to the theater since she found out about our deal last year. So far Moby and I have been able to fend her off. I have no idea why she wants to hang out with us anyway—it's not like I've ever been nice to her.

She pushes her glasses up her nose and leans down

so we're eye to eye. I try not to blink as she peers into my soul.

After a moment of the human-lie-detector routine she is satisfied that I'm lying and straightens up. "Uh-huh, that's what I thought." She folds her arms and stares some more.

I tell myself not to sweat as her bird eyes bore into me, but it's no good. Beads form on my bare head. I have to get away before some roll down into my eye. I'm an awful liar and it shows.

I start to say, "Let's go, Mo—" But when I turn, Moby is gone. He knows if we stick around, Shelby will eventually get the truth. After that, how long before we give in and let her come with us to a screening? Moby has slipped away, leaving me to deal with the flamingo.

Well played, kid.

I'm about to suggest she earn her ticket to the screening by trimming the Colonel's toenails when the intercom crackles. An earsplitting squeal is followed by the voice of our principal.

"Good moooorning, Alanmoore students. This is

Mr. Mayer." The intercom is ancient like the school, so kids move closer to hear. I know a chance to escape when I see one, so I slip away from Shelby's soul-searching stare as soon as the speaker catches her attention.

I weave my way through the crowd of students. I'm itching to get down to the pranking, but I gotta find Moby and decide what we're going to throw at the Arch next.

I hear chunks of the announcement whenever I walk near a speaker.

"Assembly . . . blah, blah . . . elections . . . blah . . ."

I know exactly where to look for Moby. He's probably in his favorite stall in the upstairs boys' room, avoiding Shelby (and everyone else) until the second bell rings. I'm starting up the staircase with my head down, deep in thought, when I run into something very dense.

"You should watch where you're going," the Arch says, pushing me away.

I catch the railing and stop myself from tumbling backward down the stairs.

"Chubby-Jet-Ski?" he asks. He knows how to say

my name. He messes it up on purpose so nobody thinks he knows me. Plus, thanks to him I'm the only bald kid in sixth grade, so who else could it be?

"What do you want?"

"From you? Nothing. I'm just surprised I didn't find a dead fish or something in my locker this morning."

I roll my eyes but also mentally add *dead fish in locker* to my list of potential pranks.

"Vill vee see you at zee assembly?" he says.

Since he turned into the Arch, he feels the need to point out my accent. The way I sound makes most people assume I'm Russian. It takes a special kind of stupid to think I sound German.

The fact that he actually acknowledged my existence to tell me about the assembly is worrisome.

"Do I have a choice?"

He thinks for a minute. "I guess not."

I try to step around him, but he moves to block me.

"Get a good seat. You're gonna want to hear real good."

"*Well*," I correct. You would think people could at least learn to speak their first language properly.

He glances past me and does a chin raise to some kids coming up the stairs. Then he eyes me like he'd probably look at a dead fish in his locker. "Whatevs, Commie!" He pushes past and high-fives the kids on the landing. I think about explaining to him that Poland is a parliamentary republic, not a Communist country, but the second bell starts ringing. More sweat forms on my head as I take the stairs. I don't like the idea of a special assembly, and I really don't like the fact that the Arch is so excited about it. He knows I've made it my mission to ruin his undeserved reputation, and he is not about to let me get away with it.

If there's one thing I know to be true, it's this: there isn't much room to hide something up your sleeve in a cutoff muscle shirt.

FOLLOW THE CLUES.
CRACK THE CODE. STAY ALIVE.